The Last People Who Knew

I0763947

While this work reflects real-world engineering concepts and operational practices, it is not intended as technical guidance or instruction. The author and publisher make no representations or warranties regarding the accuracy or completeness of any information contained herein and disclaim any liability arising from its use.

Published by Books Sphere, LLC

Grand Junction, Colorado

ISBN: 979-8-9956130-0-8

First Edition

Printed in the United States of America

This book is dedicated to the memory of

Lewis F. Gregg (1927-2019)

Dad, the seed you planted grew and produced fruit.

Thank you.

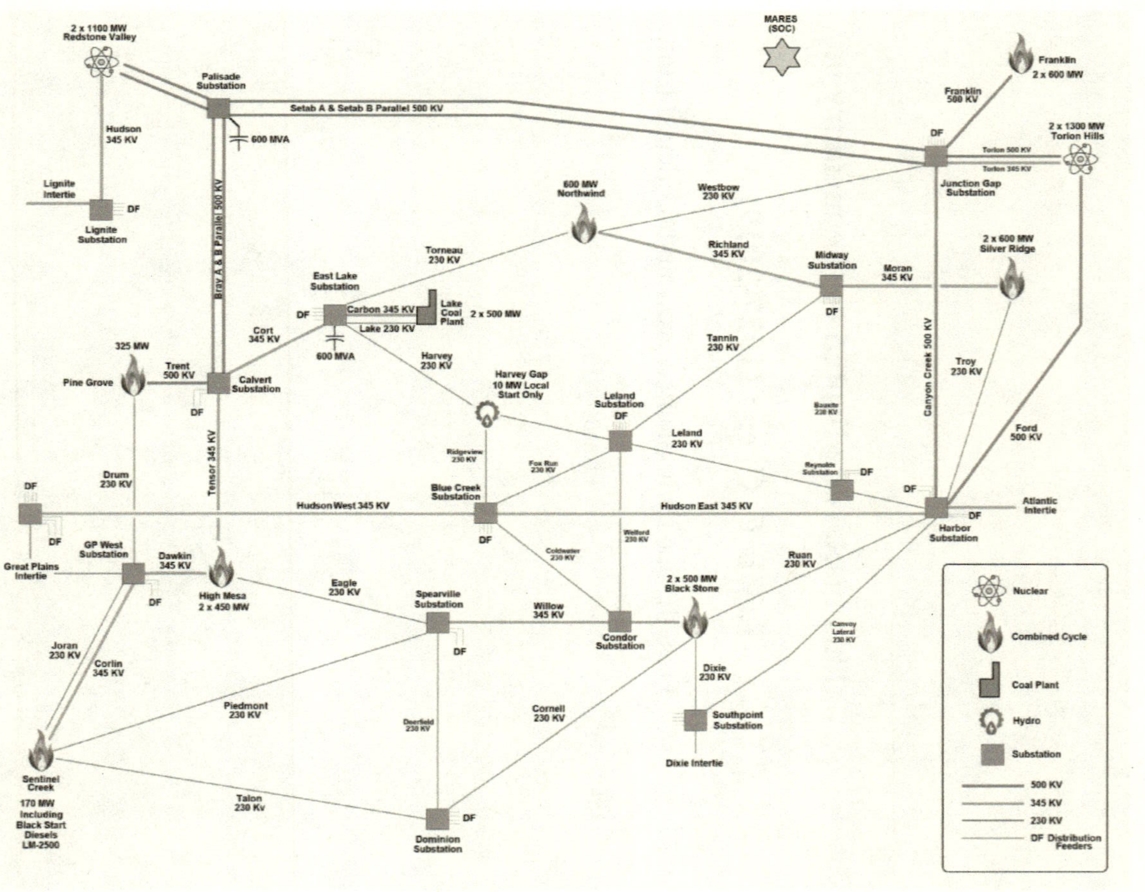

MARES (SOC)
2 x 1100 MW Redstone Valley
Palisade Substation
Setab A & Setab B Parallel 500 KV
600 MVA
Hudson 345 KV
Lignite Intertie
Lignite Substation
DF
Bray A & B Parallel 500 KV
Franklin 2 x 600 MW
Franklin 500 KV
2 x 1300 MW Torion Hills
Torion 500 KV
Torion 345 KV
Junction Gap Substation
600 MW Northwind
Westbow 230 KV
Richland 345 KV
Torneau 230 KV
East Lake Substation
Carbon 345 KV
Lake Coal Plant
2 x 500 MW
Lake 230 KV
600 MVA
Cort 345 KV
Midway Substation
Moran 345 KV
2 x 600 MW Silver Ridge
Tannin 230 KV
Troy 230 KV
Canyon Creek 500 KV
325 MW
Pine Grove
Trent 500 KV
Calvert Substation
Harvey 230 KV
Harvey Gap 10 MW Local Start Only
Leland Substation
Leland 230 KV
Reynolds Substation
Ford 500 KV
Ridgeview 230 KV
Fox Run 230 KV
Drum 230 KV
Tensor 345 KV
Blue Creek Substation
Hudson West 345 KV
Hudson East 345 KV
Atlantic Intertie
Harbor Substation
Great Plains Intertie
GP West Substation
Dawkin 345 KV
High Mesa 2 x 450 MW
Coldwater 230 KV
Wellford 230 KV
Ruan 230 KV
Eagle 230 KV
Spearville Substation
Willow 345 KV
Condor Substation
2 x 500 MW Black Stone
Joran 230 KV
Corlin 345 KV
Piedmont 230 KV
Deerfield 230 KV
Cornell 230 KV
Dixie 230 KV
Southpoint Substation
Dixie Intertie
Sentinel Creek
170 MW Including Black Start Diesels LM-2500
Talon 230 Kv
Dominion Substation
Nuclear
Combined Cycle
Coal Plant
Hydro
Substation
500 KV
345 KV
230 KV
DF Distribution Feeders

Part 1

The Trenches

****

This is a true story. Not in its names. Not in its sequence. But in its margins.

It is a story about power, not the kind that moves markets, but the kind that moves electrons. Decisions so small they barely matter, until they do.

***

Franklin Energy Center was considered the flagship of the MidAtlantic Energy combined cycle fleet. It consists of two 2×1 power blocks, four gas turbines and two steam turbines. The steam turbines are powered by Heat Recovery Steam Generators (HRSGs) that capture the waste heat from the massive gas turbines.

Though it is called "waste" heat, each HRSG supplies over 1 million pounds an hour of 1050°F steam to the steam turbine. This heat capture is what makes a combined cycle power plant over 50% efficient. A far cry from a 35% efficient coal plant. Plus, they mostly burn natural gas. Their emissions are substantially less than a coal plant of the same output.

Franklin Energy Center produces up to 1200 megawatts of power. This is enough power to supply approximately 850,000 average homes.

The glow from the large control room displays at Franklin Energy Center casts an electronic shadow behind Don Garcia, the newest operator on shift at the gas fired behemoth. He had only been in the role a few months, a consequence of the high turnover plaguing the plant.

The evening shift had started normally. Unfortunately, it didn't stay that way. He was working with Barry Johnson, the senior operator training him.

He was attempting to absorb what Barry was doing while looking for a solution in the plant operating procedures. The procedures were difficult to read because of the modifications sloppily written in the margins in every color of ink. As he perused the procedures, a steam safety valve briefly screamed defiantly in the background and reseated.

Startled, Don shot up from the console, craning his neck toward the windows overlooking the plant grounds. His grip tightened around the radio mic until his fingers blanched.

"Alex Cordon, Alex Cordon, please report to the control room ASAP."

Alarms streamed across the sixty-inch overhead display. The alarm horn wailed above them, demanding attention. The audible alarm horns and sirens were meant to alert the operator of a possible problem in the plant. Unfortunately, when things began going "south" in the control room, the alarm horns could be overwhelming and even debilitating during the stress of plant operation.

Don's voice cracked as he turned to the other operator. "Barry, is the bypass controller responding at all?"

Barry was bald, heavy, and counting the days before he could retire. Training new operators was not his first choice. Sweat had gathered on his bare scalp as he coaxed the stubborn plant controls into obedience.

"A little bit," Barry muttered. "I don't know how we are still online."

"The steam turbine megawatts are all over the map!" Don retorted. "That damn Cordon's probably with Lizzy again."

Don keyed the mic again.

"Lizzy Anderson, Lizzy Anderson."

Silence.

"Franklin Energy Center's finest," he mumbled angrily under his breath.

He was about to try again when the speaker cracked sharply.

"This is Liz. I heard a loud noise like a safety valve. Is everything okay?" She sounded alarmed.

"Have you seen Alex Cordon? We need him now."

A pause.

"I think he was in the instrument shop the last time I saw him."

Don turned to Barry, his jaw tight. Barry only grunted and shook his head, his eyes fixed on the console as he continued to wrestle with the plant controls.

Moments later, the control room door burst open. Alex Cordon sprinted in and yelled into the console area.

"What's happening?"

Don snapped.

"What have you been doing?" His voice dropped low. "Besides Liz?"

Barry jerked his head around, wondering if this was about to escalate. It was no secret that Don did not like Alex. They both thought the other was incompetent. Fortunately, Alex didn't take the bait.

"I was at the water treatment plant and didn't hear the radio. But I heard a safety blow and ran."

“The I.P. bypass has a mind of its own,” Don said, cooling his anger. “It’s throwing the steam turbine load everywhere. The I.P. steam drum level is out of control.”

An intense mechanical moan rolled through the plant, followed by a deep muffled thump. Barry immediately stiffened in his chair.

“Damn!” he growled. “The I.P. bypass went closed and then wide open,” he looked up at the display directly above him. “We just tripped on high drum level.”

Hundreds of alarms cascaded across the massive monitor. Additional alarm sirens joined the chaos.

“The gas turbines and steam turbine are offline and rolling down,” Don said after a few minutes. He was trying to sound useful but was overwhelmed. He was too new to be comfortable with a unit trip.

The grid absorbed the sudden loss of 650 megawatts without hesitation, as it had countless times before.

Alex quickly moved to the engineering station, turned the key, and began digging through screens when the phone rang. Barry jerked his head toward Don. “Answer that damn thing.”

“It was the dispatcher,” Don said after hanging up. “He wanted to know what happened. I told him Franklin Energy Center Block 1 is down until we fix the I.P. bypass. I told him we have no idea how long that will take.”

Alex kept clicking through screens. After several minutes, he slipped out of the control room unnoticed. Don and Barry were too busy stabilizing the plant.

Alex made his way to the misbehaving bypass valve, a massive, blistering-hot piece of hardware buried deep in the plant. He forced himself to focus. He checked instrument air pressure, signal strength, and loop output, anything that might explain the chaos. Nothing made sense.

He was running into the limits of what he had been taught. The community college instrumentation program had prepared him well enough to be hired, but not enough to fully understand what he was seeing.

He decided the I/P converter must be bad. It was small enough to fit in the palm of his hand and critical enough to shut down the plant. He quickly determined the warehouse didn't have the right one using the Aegis Data Management (ADM) system.

Of course it didn't.

A part that cost less than a dinner for two, and they were out of stock. Austerity measures had gutted the parts inventory in recent months. They used to stock three of everything that mattered. Now they stocked just enough to meet a spreadsheet.

He shook his head and went back to the instrumentation shop. He called a sister plant eighty miles south, the Silver Ridge Energy Center.

After being transferred, dropped, and rerouted twice, he finally reached Darren Holcomb, an Instrumentation, Control, and Electrical tech.

"Darren, this is Alex Cordon at Franklin Energy Center. I need an I/P converter for our I.P. bypass valve.

Since our plants are nearly identical, I'm hoping you've got one we can beg, borrow, or steal."

"You sure it's bad?" Darren asked. "We almost never have trouble with those. Have you checked your instrument air? What about dryer issues?"

"I looked at everything." He said impatiently. "It's definitely bad. Do you have one?"

"I'll have to check ADM and see if the warehouse has one."

Alex's voice turned cynical.

"You know what we call the ADM system here at Franklin?"

"Let me guess." Darren said. "A Damn Mess?"

"Yup."

About an hour later, Darren finally called back. No luck. They had nothing in the warehouse and since they were operating, he couldn't rob one from their plant.

It didn't matter.

Returning to the valve, Alex finally noticed the problem. Earlier he missed the feedback linkage hanging loose, barely attached. He tightened it, and worked with the operators to stroke the valve, watching it respond smoothly. After finishing, he called the control room.

"You can restart the plant. We had the parts in the warehouse, and I repaired the valve." They didn't need the full story. They just needed the plant back.

Raises and bonuses had become skimpy to non-existent. Equipment was pushed harder every year. The warehouse shelves grew sparse, and company vehicle lifespans were extended indefinitely.

Employee morale and turnover were moving opposite to each other. As morale decreased, the turnover increased. Not surprising nor unexpected. Shifts were filled with personnel that were not confident in their knowledge and abilities. Reliability began to suffer. Not badly, but the metrics were decreasing. The slide was slow enough the plant personnel hardly noticed.

This time, the unit would be back online in a few hours. Another trip, another quiet repair. No one would remember it a year later.

These things had been set in motion at MidAtlantic Energy three years earlier.

***

Part 2

Warren Buffton

****

For nearly thirty years, Warren Buffton had been known in financial circles as the Oracle of Overland. Overland, Kansas was far from Wall Street, and his nickname had nothing to do with power plants. It had been earned in quieter arenas: insurance float, disciplined acquisitions, and capital placed where others hesitated.

He was patient but moved with conviction when the numbers aligned. While others chased quarterly applause, Buffton studied balance sheets and human behavior. He thought in decades rather than quarters. He preferred businesses that produced something real, something people could not live without. Railroads. Insurance. Energy. The less glamorous the better. Those industries offered predictable cash flow, durable demand, and competent management. That was enough for him.

Utilities entered his orbit long after his reputation had settled into the financial press. To Warren, utilities resembled railroads. They were immense capital already sunk into the ground, protected by regulation, and paid for slowly by millions of customers who could not simply choose to stop using electricity. He certainly did not pretend to understand combustion dynamics or grid stability. That was not his expertise. His expertise was capital allocation.

Buffton believed in hiring competent people and letting them do their jobs to the best of their ability. He felt that intelligent, disciplined leadership, properly incentivized and minimally interfered with, could run almost anything. The formula had worked for him repeatedly.

MidAtlantic Energy was simply the latest expression of that philosophy. Several large utilities gathered beneath one disciplined umbrella. A steady hand, a rational board, and a promise never to gamble with shareholder money.

Buffton did not see himself as a conqueror of complex systems. He saw himself as a steward of capital. If weaknesses existed inside the machinery, the professionals would find and correct them.

It was a reasonable assumption. But assumptions, like turbines, operate within tolerances. Once exceeded, they do not negotiate.

Buffton's philosophy was disarmingly simple. *Never lose money.* Once the acquisitions were complete, he did what he always did. He installed leadership he trusted to preserve the numbers. Profits did not require affection. They required discipline.

For MidAtlantic, he selected a juggernaut. Stephen Langford was forty-three years old, confident, and unmistakably intelligent. He had moved through the corporate world like a force of nature. Harvard Law had not held his interest for long; high finance had. His ascent had been rapid, COO, then CFO, and now a candidate for CEO of MidAtlantic Energy, one of the ten largest utilities in the country.

Buffton invited him to Overland to meet with the board. As always, Stephen did his homework.

The board had quietly discussed one other candidate, the sitting CEO of Viking Energy Corporation. Several directors favored him. Warren did not. He believed the future required something different. Stephen Langford was second on a very short list.

The meeting room that afternoon was quiet but charged with expectation.

“Thank you for coming, Stephen,” Warren said, gesturing toward the board members seated around the table. “You’ve probably guessed why we invited you.”

Stephen nodded.

“You’re assembling MidAtlantic Energy.”

Warren smiled faintly.

“Nothing escapes you.”

“I try not to let it,” Stephen replied confidently.

“We’re bringing together several underperforming assets,” Warren continued. “They need disciplined leadership. Someone who can turn structure into performance.”

Stephen leaned slightly forward.

“Warren, esteemed board members, that is what I do.”

Warren studied him for a moment before speaking again.

“You do not have utility experience.”

“No,” Stephen said evenly.

“But you do have a strong record for returns and leadership.” Warren paused. “The only concern raised by the board involves Aegis Data Management. I believe it is commonly called ADM. That episode drew attention.”

Stephen’s expression did not change.

“I was cleared of any wrongdoing,” he said. “The accusations came from a director who was later proven corrupt. My mistake was trusting someone whose reputation appeared sound."

Warren held his gaze.

"Do you still own shares of this company?"

"I do not currently hold any shares of ADM. As I said, I was cleared of all improprieties."

The board remained silent. A few members exchanged brief glances and nodded almost imperceptibly.

Finally Warren spoke again.

"We would like you to take the helm of MidAtlantic Energy and lead it out of the financial wilderness."

He paused.

"Are you interested in that challenge?"

Stephen sat motionless for a moment.

Then he nodded once.

"I would consider it both an honor and a challenge," he said. "One I intend to succeed at."

Stephen Langford's appointment made national business headlines. Inside MidAtlantic, his presence was felt almost immediately. At first he moved quietly, studying the organization. Then the changes began. Careers accelerated. Others ended abruptly. The early changes were subtle but unmistakable. Meetings grew shorter. Reports grew thinner. Managers who spoke in cautious abstractions found themselves replaced by people who spoke in numbers.

Within months, his reputation inside the company was summarized in a single unspoken understanding: *Resistance was futile.*

Competence was expected. Loyalty was assumed. Those who failed either standard did not remain part of the team.

Langford was not widely liked. He was respected. It was almost universally agreed that he was brilliant, and ruthless.

Some believed his severity was necessary, that MidAtlantic needed to be shaken free from old school complacency. Others believed he was dismantling what wasn't broken simply to prove he could… It was just another stepping stone to prove his brilliance. Langford didn't care what they believed. Results were what mattered. By every visible measure, he always delivered.

Within days of taking the helm of MidAtlantic, he summoned the entire top management team to the boardroom. The tension was thick that day. Rumors had spread through every level of the company that "Mr." Langford was not pleased. Change was coming, and it would be fast.

Michael Orenstein, the long term and widely respected Chief Operating Officer, opened that fateful meeting that began the company redirection.

"To my colleagues at MidAtlantic, thank you for joining us. We're entering a new era in U.S. power generation. Our challenges have never been greater. We face increasing renewable penetration, tightening margins, and financial pressure from independent power producers." He paused. "We're fortunate to have one of the nation's best taking the helm. For those who haven't met him, I'd like to introduce Mr. Stephen Langford."

Polite, restrained applause followed.

"Thank you, Michael," Langford said. He cleared his throat.

He let the room settle, scanning the faces of all thirty-five senior managers and directors. He didn't smile.

"I'm opening with a simple question," he began. "We operate two large nuclear plants, one of the nation's larger coal plants, and seven large combined-cycle gas facilities. In my first few days here, I've determined our staffing is significantly higher than every peer company I've reviewed."

No one moved. A few stared at their notepads.

"Our Torlon Hills nuclear station, two units and 2,600 megawatts, has one hundred twenty more employees than at least three comparable plants."

He took a sip of water.

“Franklin Energy Center and Silver Ridge Energy Center are each 1,200-megawatt combined-cycle facilities. Between them, we carry a staggering 172 people.”

He looked slowly around the room allowing his words to penetrate.

“Our largest competitor in this region is NovaCore Power. I’m sure you’ve all heard of them.”

A faint ripple of nervous laughter moved through the room.

“NovaCore operates a plant nearly identical to Franklin or Silver Ridge,” Langford said. “They report forty-three full-time personnel onsite. Their operating metrics match or exceed ours.” He let the silence stretch. “Why?”

No one answered immediately. Several managers shifted in their chairs. One quietly closed a notebook. The question was simple. The answer was not.

Hillary Serraldi, Senior Vice President of Human Resources, finally raised her hand and spoke boldly. She dealt extensively with this subject in recent years.

"Their personnel numbers are deeply skewed. NovaCore incorporates substantial use of contractors for routine and breakdown maintenance. We made a corporate decision to keep core functions in-house. It's cleaner. We control performance. There's less legal ambiguity."

Langford slowly nodded once and stared directly at her.

"That's interesting," he said. "Because NovaCore's profits are higher than ours. Their safety record is as good as ours, some would say better, and their availability metrics match or exceed ours."

A dark silence filled the room.

Hillary tried again. "NovaCore operates only combined cycle and renewables. They don't carry the burden of nuclear oversight or an aging coal plant. Are we comparing apples to apples here?"

Langford studied her. He wasn't angry or offended. He was simply evaluating.

"This thinking ends now," he said.

Again, he allowed his words to settle.

"We will move beyond old paradigms that feel comfortable and produce poor results. We will optimize operations around profitability and performance. Additional personnel does not automatically create more safety. Additional personnel does not automatically create better productivity. Stop telling yourselves that it does. Our thinking must change."

He paused.

"I've reviewed the salary bands for every single person in this room. MidAtlantic is paying quite a handsome premium for leadership." His eyes moved from face to face. "That suggests I should be looking at a room full of intelligent, aggressive thinkers."

No one reacted.

"Each of you has 96 hours to rewrite the operating model for your area and present it to me personally."

The tone was set. MidAtlantic would move.

The coming days found most of the managers reluctant to present their cost cutting measures to Stephen Langford. However, none were more pensive than Joel Adamson.

Joel was the Senior Vice President of Transmission and Distribution for MidAtlantic. He handled the "wires". His job was to ensure the grid connections with the Mid-Atlantic & Regional Energy System (MARES) power pool were properly managed. This was no small task.

Due to the massive cost and legal barriers to building new transmission lines, the grid was undersized and frequently operating near capacity across the entire region. On most days the margins were thin but manageable. On the wrong day, they would disappear entirely. The addition of a sizable portion of renewables didn't help, either.

Joel was an electrical engineer with a reputation for being inconveniently correct. He had spent twenty years studying transmission system issues most executives never thought about. That habit had made him valuable. It had also made him unpopular on numerous occasions.

Joel's ascent to the VP position was clawed out of unwavering competence. Most remembered his head-on collision with his former boss and VP, Norman Tullman. Joel announced to his face in an open meeting that he was, "Patently wrong."

Concerning a major grid security issue that Joel had been warning as many as would listen. Less than a week later a presumed group of North Korean hackers managed to partially open the 500 kV north corridor by breaking into the SCADA telemetry system.

The North Koreans' mistake? They broke into the system during a temperate spring day when demand was low enough that the system absorbed the loss without a massive upset.

Utilities across the region had quietly sought Joel's advice when transmission problems grew complicated. He had never once softened an answer to make it easier to hear. In recent years he had received several industry awards for handling complex grid problems.

Today, he knew he must stand tall and present the "bad news" to Stephen exactly as he had with Norman Tullman over grid security. The bad news? Not only would there not be any budget cuts in his area, he required over two hundred million dollars just to "catch-up".

Joel and Stephen's meeting started cordially. Keeping with his reputation, Stephen did his homework on Joel before the meeting. He knew he was a good engineer. He had also heard he was a forthright, no-bullshit manager. This could be good or bad depending on what Stephen's objective of the day was. It did not take long for Joel to drop his bomb.

"Stephen, you will see in my extensive documentation package that we are behind the eight ball in a number of areas." Joel was not going to soften the blow. He didn't know how. He was a good engineer and facts were facts, numbers were numbers, the need was clearly proven.

"We have two 1,500 MVA transformers at Torlon Hills nuclear plant, one 750 MVA transformer at Lakeside Coal Plant, and one 1450 MVA transformer at Redstone Valley Nuclear Plant that are generating gas. We MUST look at replacements."

Stephen never flinched. He had questions, though.

"I am not an electrical engineer. Translate this for me."

"MVA stands for megavolt-amps. It's the electrical capacity of the transformer." He tightened his face. "These are HUGE transformers. Each of them is called a GSU, or Generator Step-Up Transformer, and is connected to the main generator in the plant." He studied Stephen's face for a sign of comprehension. "They connect the generators at the plant to the grid at much higher voltage."

"What do you mean they are generating gas?" Stephen asked in a puzzled tone.

"These massive transformers have complex cooling systems. The windings in the transformer are oil submerged, and this oil is circulated and cooled externally. When excessive heat or electrical arcing occurs inside the transformer windings, the cooling oil produces hydrogen. I'm sure you understand how explosive that can be."

"Is this not manageable?"

"It is to a degree. However, fault-arcing produces acetylene which is more explosive than hydrogen. Have you ever seen an online video of one of these transformers exploding? It is spectacular. It can send a mushroom cloud 300 or 400 feet in the air. When they fail, they do not simply trip offline. They destroy everything around them."

Joel grimaced before continuing.

"These transformers will require replacement at some point. Due to their age and winding breakdown, we should be ordering the transformers now. They have a two year or longer lead time at approximately 20 million dollars per transformer. It's all in my report."

Stephen suppressed his irritation.

"Why have we not done anything prior to this?"

Joel looked straight at him steely eyed.

"Budget cuts and shortfalls. No one wants to hear this because it is not a guaranteed failure. We've called it managed risk, but we are leaving that realm and heading for catastrophic failure."

Stephen pondered for a moment before coldly replying.

"I will read your report. We may have to discuss this further when I am complete."

"I'm not done. There is more bad news not fully expounded in my report."

"Continue." Stephen was growing impatient.

"We have severe line-loading issues. At least one of the two units at Torlon Hills is a must-run unit to control VARs and power factor. Also, at least one unit at Lakeside is a must-run. Plus, we have two additional combined cycle units where at least one block must run for VAR and power factor support." Joel paused and looked in Stephen's eyes to see if his news registered.

"VAR and power factor support is sometimes called voltage support. Our system has issues maintaining the proper voltage to the customers. We have already been fined by MARES. We put a band-aid on the situation using a large phase-shift transformer we took from one of the retired coal plants." Joel paused to ensure he was making his point.

"I must stress to you that the phase-shift transformer was barely a band-aid just to keep MARES off our back. Under the right conditions, we could suffer a voltage problem that could produce a total grid collapse."

Stephen was no longer listening.

"I will read your report. Thanks for coming in. I will contact you when I have sufficient information to discuss it further."

Joel quietly left the office.

Neither of them understood what had just begun. Deep in the MidAtlantic system, the transformers Joel had mentioned continued humming quietly under load.

***

Part 3

Change

****

Stephen Langford never stayed still for long. He moved quickly, made decisions early, and rarely revisited them. In meetings he tended to speak last, not because he wasn't listening, but because he had already decided what he was going to do.

After several days reviewing Joel Adamson's documentation on transformers, VAR support, and grid constraints, Langford acted. He asked for Kendall Allen.

Kendall Allen was an electrical engineer working in nuclear fuel management. He was young, aggressive, and technically competent. He did not like being called "Ken." That name was too common. His family and friends knew to call him Kendall.

He was the third of eight children. His parents quietly celebrated him as their "gifted" child. They were not quiet enough. It created resentment among his siblings, especially his oldest brother, Arlyss. They had been at odds since their earliest memories.

Kendall's father repaired appliances for a living. His mother had the far more demanding task of managing eight energetic children.

His father favored Kendall, partly because the boy understood things quickly. Kendall absorbed mechanical and electrical ideas almost instinctively. One moment from childhood never left him.

He was seven years old, standing in the yard beside his father while a garden hose ran across the grass. His father turned on the faucet and the hose stiffened slightly as water surged through it. His father lifted the hose.

"This hose is like an electrical conductor," he said. "The hose is the wire. The water inside it is what we call current, or amperage. It's the substance moving through the wire."

Kendall watched the water surge out of the open end.

"The pressure pushing the water through the hose," his father continued, "that's like voltage. Voltage is like electrical pressure."

He shut the water off, connected another hose to the first one, and turned the faucet back on.

"Now watch," he said. "The farther the water travels in the hose, the less pressure you get at the end. That's like resistance in an electrical circuit."

Kendall was hooked from that day forward. To him, electricity was a hidden force that ran the world. He could not get enough of it.

Many years later he graduated summa cum laude in electrical engineering. He remained close to his dad. He never patched things up with Arlyss. The eldest Allen child felt Kendall wasn't gifted, he was simply arrogant.

Kendall's ambition had few limits. Most people who knew him understood his agenda: move vertically as fast as possible. He had a reputation at Torlon Hills and Redstone Valley nuclear plants for volunteering aggressively and advancing just as quickly. His name appeared often in internal discussions about "high potential" personnel.

He entered Langford's office without hesitation. The room was large but sparsely decorated. A single framed financial chart hung behind the desk where most executives displayed awards or photographs. Kendall crossed the room confidently and shook the CEO's hand with a firmness that bordered on arrogance.

"Kendall," Langford said, motioning him to a chair. "You're probably wondering why you're here."

"Yes, sir," Kendall said, meeting his gaze.

"I'm reorganizing several departments," Langford said. "The goal is efficiency. Lower cost. Faster decision-making." He paused. "I'm looking for people who aren't burdened by old assumptions. People who move."

Kendall nodded once. "I definitely believe in outcomes," he said.

Langford smiled, studying him for a moment. He knew he had the right man.

"Would you be willing to accept a Senior Vice President role and take over Transmission and Distribution for MidAtlantic?"

Kendall blinked twice.

"Yes," he said immediately. "Absolutely."

"I expected that," Langford said. "Your salary range will increase substantially, and I will leave this conversation between you and human resources."

Kendall was stunned by the appointment. He had worked for this moment since entering the corporate world, but felt it was still several years away.

Stephen smiled, stood and held out his hand to Kendall.

"This will be effective next Monday. You'll need to relocate. All relevant personnel and directors will be notified today."

Kendall stood, shook Langford's hand again.

"Thank you, Mr. Langford. I can assure you I will not let you down."

"Please, my vice presidents all call me Stephen."

Kendall smiled broadly.

"Thank you, Stephen."

He left the large, opulent office excited and visibly energized.

A few minutes later, Langford placed another call. This time to Joel Adamson.

"Joel, this is Stephen Langford," he said. "I'm reassigning you."

There was a pause on the line.

"Providing you accept it, I would like you to become the Senior Vice President of Grid Integration," Langford continued. "It's a new role built from Harry

Halvorsen's former scope. It is the same work, but cleaner reporting. It is strategically important. Because of this, I want your energy, competence, and experience applied there."

Joel said nothing at first.

"And transmission and distribution?" he asked flatly.

"I've made other arrangements," Langford said. "I trust you'll transition quickly."

Harry Halvorsen had run Systems Reliability through three mergers. His work focused on long-range hardening, adaptation strategy, and the unglamorous task of preserving operating margins. His plans were methodical, capital-intensive, and stubbornly resistant to short-term measurement. Not long after Stephen's arrival, this division was consolidated into "integration" for efficiency.

Later that afternoon, word circulated that Harry, a highly compensated director with years of institutional memory, was leaving with a severance package. No announcement followed. No explanation was offered. Everyone already knew what had happened. His corporate entrance badge worked until it didn't.

After the call ended, Joel sat alone in his office, reeling. He understood the move for what it was. It wasn't a demotion. It wasn't a promotion. It was efficient, clean *removal.*

Joel pondered the new position. He had spent twenty-two years inside the preceding mergers that eventually became MidAtlantic. His compensation package was generous and his reputation intact. He decided he would accept it quietly. Still, the way it had been done stayed with him.

Kendall Allen began his oversight of the Transmission and Distribution department with little fanfare. He had only been in the position a little over a week when he was invited into Stephen's office again.

"It is good to see you, Kendall. Are you getting settled, okay?"

"Yes, sir. The staff has been very helpful and accommodating. I am leaning on Joel Adamson for insight. His experience in this area has been very helpful."

"Good. I felt you would come up to speed quickly." He reached across the desk and handed Kendall a printed spreadsheet.

"This is your department's transmission and distribution budget for the past ten years. I know you have been moving in many directions, but I want to discuss the financial future of your portion of this company."

Kendall puffed up slightly as he scanned the figures. Stephen didn't let him fully finish before looking at him intently and declaring, "As you can see, I would like to rein in the spending on transmission and distribution, but your predecessor was quite resistive."

"I believe Joel had some legitimate concerns, sir."

"Please call me Stephen. We are a team. I want you to think that way." He paused. "Now concerning Joel's concerns, you told me you believed in outcomes during our first meeting. I would like you to challenge the status quo and work through the issues Joel raised. Do two things."

He leaned forward slightly and lowered his voice.

"I want you to keep us operating safely and efficiently, and do so within the financial constraints I am proposing."

Kendall shifted in his chair and looked again at the spreadsheet. Before he could answer, Stephen continued.

"I am asking you to engage your highly capable intelligence and do what Joel was unable or unwilling to do. Find the answers using engineering expertise and your staff, not just by dumping piles of money on the problem."

Kendall raised his eyebrows and glanced at the current year numbers again. His instincts told him the capital allocation was thin. Still, he answered carefully.

"I will do my very best. As you may know, I saved MidAtlantic several million dollars in nuclear fuel management. I may be able to do the same here."

"That's all I can ask." Stephen smiled warmly. "I am certain I picked the right man."

It took Kendall several months to reduce the budget enough to earn Stephen's approval. Joel Adamson's list of critical infrastructure needs was never fully prioritized. In time, most of it simply slipped from the center of discussion.

Kendall was not careless. He monitored the transmission system closely, working with his engineers to establish action and alert levels for emerging equipment issues. Each situation had margins and response windows. If a parameter moved beyond its expected range, there would still be time to react.

Stephen liked what he saw. Kendall appeared efficient and disciplined in his oversight. For a while, it worked.

Two years passed without a major incident on the grid. Transformers were aging and occasionally troublesome, but they remained in service. Kendall reviewed their reports regularly and consulted with knowledgeable engineers when something looked unusual.

He had several long conversations with Joel Adamson during that period. Kendall liked Joel and respected him. Joel was a meticulous engineer who understood the grid as a living system. Kendall did not entirely disagree with Joel's concerns about slow deterioration in parts of the network. But Stephen's words stayed with him. Engage your intelligence. Solve the problem. Don't just spend money.

Kendall believed there was wisdom in that. Indiscriminately pouring money into a system did not necessarily improve it. Often it simply made the system more expensive.

Occasionally Kendall found himself thinking about his father.

His dad had been a capable appliance repairman. Nothing fancy. Just practical and methodical. Kendall remembered one afternoon when a neighbor, Jerry

McClelland, had called in desperation. Jerry's washing machine had failed, but his wife was fighting cancer and the family was nearly bankrupt.

Kendall went with his father on the service call. Normally a repair like that meant replacing the entire pump assembly. Instead, his father removed the pump, replaced a small seal, and reassembled it with careful precision. The part cost two dollars.

On the drive home his father said something Kendall never forgot.

"Most of the time we replace the whole pump. It's faster and safer. But sometimes you can fix the small thing that's actually broken. It may take a little extra work, but it saves over a hundred dollars."

Kendall remembered the transformer reports sitting on his desk the next morning. Sometimes a system didn't need to be rebuilt. Sometimes it only needed careful attention.

He continued reviewing the transformer diagnostics. In several cases, the insulating oil analyses showed subtle increases in dissolved gases. The numbers were not yet high enough to trigger the alarm thresholds he had set. Not yet.

The reports were filed. Trend lines were updated. The transformers remained in service and carefully watched.

Reactive power loading across the major transmission corridors was also being closely managed. The "must-run" generating units were rotated through required maintenance cycles so that voltage support was always available when needed. Within those constraints, Kendall met the target budget goals.

Stephen continued hiring outside efficiency consultants to examine every department within MidAtlantic. Each report pushed the company a little further toward becoming what Stephen called a lean, disciplined energy enterprise.

Two years later the results were undeniable. The balance sheet looked excellent. Across the grid, however, several pieces of equipment were now operating closer to their limits than anyone outside Kendall's department fully understood.

***

Part 4

Show and Tell

****

The Hudson 345 kV transmission line corridor ran through three states and more than two hundred miles of farmland, forest, and river valley. Most people who drove beneath the towers never noticed them. They were simply part of the background of modern life, steel skeletons marching across the landscape in quiet formation.

To the operators inside MidAtlantic's transmission control center, Hudson was something else entirely. It was a problem.

On the operations floor, the night shift had settled into the familiar rhythm that came after midnight. Coffee cups accumulated near keyboards. Conversations were short and technical.

A young transmission operator named Kyle Patterson leaned forward toward his screen.

"Hudson East is climbing again."

The senior operator beside him did not look up immediately.

"How high?"

"Ninety-three percent."

That finally got his attention.

"Which direction?"

"West to east."

The senior operator frowned slightly. Winter peaks usually flowed the other way. Cities along the coast consumed enormous amounts of electricity, but tonight something upstream was pushing power harder than usual.

"Check the Canyon Creek tie."

Kyle pulled up the numbers.

"Canyon's already at ninety-six."

The senior operator leaned back and studied the wall display. Colored transmission corridors stretched across the digital map like arteries, Everything was still green. Green meant normal. But green could be misleading.

"Call generation dispatch," he said. "See if they can back anything down west of Hudson."

Kyle made the call. The answer came back quickly.

"Nothing available. Everything already committed."

The senior operator nodded. That was not surprising. Utilities had been trimming reserve margins for years. Across the room another operator spoke up.

"We're getting some wind alarms up north."

"Ice?"

"Looks like it."

That got everyone's attention. Ice did two things to transmission lines. It added weight and changed the electrical characteristics of the conductors. Most of the time the system absorbed it without much trouble. Most of the time.

"How bad?" the senior operator asked.

"Too early to tell."

He looked again at the Hudson corridor. Ninety-three percent loading was not dangerous by itself.

Transmission lines were designed with safety margins. But safety margins assumed the rest of the system behaved normally. He tapped the screen lightly.

"Keep an eye on Hudson."

Kyle nodded. Outside the control center the storm continued to build across the northern corridor. Freezing rain coated the lattice towers and collected along the conductors in thick, clear sleeves. The lines sagged slightly under the growing weight.

Inside the control room the loading climbed to ninety-four percent. No alarms sounded. The system was still green.

***

Dale Morrison was studying a Condition Report on a recurring valve actuator failure when the phone rang. It was the third time the component had appeared in the plant's corrective action system in six months. He read the report again before answering. Recurring problems were rarely about the part that failed. They meant something else had been missed.

The office was quiet except for the low hum of ventilation and the distant mechanical rhythm of Torlon Hills Nuclear Plant operating beyond the walls. Twenty-six hundred megawatts of electricity, enough to power about two million homes, flowed from this plant.

Inside the plant manager's office the world was reduced to paperwork, engineering reports, and the occasional unpleasant phone call.

Dale let the phone ring once more before picking it up.

"Morrison."

"Dale, it's Cal."

Calvin Johnson was MidAtlantic's Vice President of Nuclear, a position he occupied largely because Stephen Langford trusted him.

Cal had spent most of his career as a corporate attorney. He was very good at it. During law school he discovered he had a talent for navigating complex legal problems and an even greater talent for keeping powerful people out of trouble.

That ability was how he first met Stephen Langford years earlier during Langford's aggressive takeover of Aegis Data Management. The acquisition had been controversial and tangled in accusations of insider trading and regulatory maneuvering that briefly attracted the attention of several federal agencies.

Cal had stepped in quietly. Within months Langford's legal problems had evaporated. The two men developed an easy professional relationship built on loyalty and mutual usefulness. When Langford later became CEO of MidAtlantic, Cal followed him. Officially, Cal was first appointed Chief Legal Counsel. Unofficially, he had become Langford's fixer.

When MidAtlantic's previous Vice President of Nuclear abruptly resigned to "pursue other opportunities," Langford filled the vacancy with someone he trusted.

Calvin Johnson. Cal knew the law very well. Nuclear power, not so much.

Dale leaned back slightly in his chair. Cal never called without a reason.

"What's going on, Cal?"

"We're going to need some of your time next week," Cal said. "We've got a high-level political delegation from Indonesia coming through Torlon Hills."

Dale closed the Condition Report and waited.

"Warren Buffton is trying to develop business with them," Cal continued. "They're moving toward nuclear power and Warren smells opportunity. He'll be here along with Stephen Langford and a group of Indonesian political leaders. Press, cameras, the whole circus."

Dale sighed quietly.

"You want a tour."

"You guessed it."

Dale glanced across his desk at the neat stacks of engineering reports waiting for attention.

"That's fine. How deep do you want to go? Fluff or substance?"

"Pull out all the stops," Cal said. "We're catering lunch in that big conference room of yours. Press will be everywhere. Warren and Stephen want them to see the simulator and the actual plant control room. They're pushing the idea that the simulator is identical to the real thing."

Dale paused.

"Cal, do I need to remind you that NRC access authorization requirements include documented background checks and psychological evaluations? That process exists for a reason."

Cal groaned.

"Dale, I'm told you're the best nuclear plant manager a company could hope for. I mean that. But sometimes you need to pull the stick out of your ass."

Dale laughed softly.

"This is from an attorney with a legal pole permanently installed?"

Cal ignored the remark and continued. "We're talking about Buffton, Langford, and the leaders of a friendly country," Cal said. "We're not letting them run the reactor."

Dale rubbed his temple.

"I remember now," he said dryly. "Rules apply except when they don't."

"You can be an asshole when you want to be," Cal said.

"Comes with the job."

There was a brief pause.

"We'll be ready," Dale said. "I'll make sure everything is shipshape."

They hung up. Dale sat for a moment before reopening the Condition Report. Corporate visits were rarely about engineering. They were about appearances.

Dale Morrison had spent six years in the Navy's nuclear propulsion program before ever setting foot inside a civilian power plant. His parents had imagined a very different path for him.

His mother was a vascular surgeon. His father was a mechanical engineer and proud graduate of Rensselaer Polytechnic Institute. Engineering discussions had been normal dinner conversation while he was growing up.

Precision ran in the family. His grandfather held patents for automatic transmission components. A great-great-grandfather had been a mathematician and amateur astronomer.

Dale had two older sisters. One became an accomplished pianist. The other followed their mother into medicine. Both seemed to know exactly what they wanted from life. Dale had not.

During his junior and senior years of high school he developed a stubborn streak of rebellion fueled largely by his parents' insistence that he attend Rensselaer like his father. A week after graduation the argument finally reached its conclusion. Dale packed a bag, walked out of the house, and enlisted in the United States Navy for six years with a contract for nuclear power training.

His parents were devastated.

Dale explained it simply. He wanted to see more of the world than classrooms could offer while still working inside the discipline of engineering.

Six years in the nuclear Navy stripped away both his rebellion and his illusions. Dale excelled there. After "A" school he trained on the S5W land-based prototype reactor. The reactor obeyed laws that never negotiated and never cared about opinion. Dale found an odd and satisfying comfort in that.

After nuclear power school he reported to a fast-attack submarine where imagination had little operational value and excuses had none at all. The plant demanded precision. It suited him.

Months at sea left a man with plenty of time to think. Dale eventually realized he wanted more than a life inside steel pressure hulls. When his enlistment ended, he used the GI Bill to attend Purdue University.

He approached engineering school the way the Navy had trained him. Show up early. Do the work. Leave systems better than you found them.

Dale joined Torlon Hills as a junior engineer shortly after graduating. He advanced steadily through the ranks, not because he courted favor, but because when equipment failed he understood it, and when decisions were required he made them.

Politics exist inside every large organization. Dale avoided them whenever possible.

His greatest strength was also his most unforgiving flaw. The plant came first. Always. He believed a nuclear station owed the public nothing less than perfection. Over time that conviction narrowed his world. Carla thought she had married a handsome, capable, ambitious man. She had married a nuclear plant.

Dale rarely noticed the quieter signs of failure at home. He was usually at the plant.

After a particularly difficult run of non-stop days during an outage Dale decided to come home at noon and surprise Carla by taking her to lunch. He was the one who was surprised.

The divorce was efficient and painful. He felt like a fool because he didn't even see it coming.

News of the big visit spread through the plant within hours. There was an open call for overtime for the rest of the week. Cleaning crews were writing their own ticket. Maintenance teams that normally struggled to get approval for spare parts suddenly had authorization for cosmetic repairs. Handrails were repainted. Floor markings were redone. The cracked tiles outside the control room, ignored for years, were finally replaced. Even long-ignored light fixtures were repaired.

The simulator suite received a full cleaning. One supervisor quietly removed three active Condition Reports from the whiteboard in the control room before the tour group arrived. They would be returned afterward.

By Wednesday the administrative wing, simulator rooms, and control room areas looked better than they had in years. Better, several operators joked, than they had looked when the plant first synchronized to the grid.

Dale watched the activity with mild amusement. Corporate visits had a way of motivating people, even when nothing important had actually changed.

Wednesday of the next week both blocks at Silver Ridge unexpectedly came offline. They had thrust bearing issues on the steam turbine for block – 1, and block – 2 had a second main oil pump fail, the primary had been out of service for weeks, leaving them with only the emergency DC oil pump before the unit tripped. The grid, as usual, absorbed and compensated for the hundreds of lost megawatts but line loading and voltage control was very problematic.

The grid was built for power to be spread across dozens of stations. When too much generation disappears in one place, electricity crowds the remaining paths. Voltages wander. Lines run hot. Dispatchers call and ask for favors nobody wants to grant. This, along with unplanned maintenance issues at three other plants, caused severe line loading issues from the south side of the grid. It forced Torlon Hills to 50% power operation on both units. Even then, the voltage/VAR loading was way out of whack. No problem. The tour was still on.

Thursday arrived and proved to be a circus. One of the richest men in the world and his hand-picked titans of industry/finance were there. High ranking political officials from Indonesia were there and the press was having a heyday.

An opulent lunch was served. The smiles, both real and disingenuous, were incessant. Dale was now “up” and put into “infotainment” mode. He moved into the massive simulator room with the lethargic, smiling delegation.

“Gentlemen, it is an honor to host you here at our Torlon Hills nuclear plant. We have been safely and efficiently generating power for the New England and Mid-Atlantic regions for over thirty years.”

The delegation spread out into the jungle of lights, meters, switches, and displays. Dale gently herded them toward the large reactor control rod mimic, raising his hand toward it while facing them.

“This is the heart of reactor control. The control rods indicated on this matrix absorb neutrons and suppress the nuclear reaction when they are inserted into the core. As they are withdrawn, reactor power increases, heating the ultra-pure water circulating through the vessel. That heat is transferred in the steam generators, where steam is produced and sent to the turbine to drive the generator.”

Eko Nugroho, a technical advisor to the Indonesian delegation, raised his hand.

“Mr. Dale. How is reactor power regulated once critical, if you can explain please? Thank you, sir.”

“No problem.” Dale stepped closer to read his name badge. He had known an Indonesian engineer at Purdue University named Nugroho. Sharp as a tack. A good man.

“Once the reactor is critical, fine power control is handled primarily through boron concentration in the coolant. Boron acts as a neutron absorber. Control rods provide coarse control and shape the flux in the core, but chemistry does most of the steady work.”

Dale gently directed them past the reactor feed pumps, then the steam generator feed pumps, and finally toward the turbine and generator controls. The delegation lingered, seemingly mesmerized by the complexity and the sheer number of instruments.

Dale had always believed that the most dangerous problems inside large machines were the quiet ones. Turbines did not usually fail dramatically without warning. They whispered first. A vibration trace that crept a little higher each month. A bearing temperature that required slightly more explanation than the last outage report had provided.

Engineers watched those numbers the way sailors watched weather. Sometimes the storm passed. Sometimes it didn't.

Torlon Hills' Unit 1 turbine had been whispering for months. The engineering staff believed they understood the problem. Dale believed them. For the moment, belief was all anyone had.

After answering several more questions, primarily from Eko Nugroho, Cal suggested they transition to the main plant control room.

Dale shuddered. He still did not like this idea. He decided to make one final check to ensure the plant was running properly before moving them to the control room. He called the Chief Shift Engineer, Billy Moss, from the simulator room phone and lowered his voice.

“Billy, this is Dale. We are ready to come to the control room. Can you give me any reason why this is a bad time?”

“I can! Our quick descent in power yesterday has unit – 1 fighting Xenon concentration in the reactor. We are so close to the refueling outage that we may be stuck here until the outage.”

Dale grimaced.

“Billy, we already discussed this. Is there an acute reason why we can’t come up there right now?”

“No. We are dealing with that vibration issue when the load on the turbine is under 800 megwatts, but it is holding right below alarm point. We should be good.”

Dale hung up the phone, smiled hesitantly, and invited the delegation to accompany him to the control room. He stopped them at the security entrance and, yelling over the din of the main turbine, gave them a final warning. “Gentlemen, let me remind you, we are entering the actual control room of an operating nuclear plant. This is not a simulator. Please keep your distance from the control boards."

It made no sense to him, bringing them here. By design and NRC mandate, the room looked identical to the simulator they had just left. After the group badged through the bulky security doors, Dale explained the roles of the Chief Shift Engineer, the Senior Reactor Operator (SRO), and the Reactor Operators (RO).

Upon entering, they moved toward the main control boards for Unit 1. The large megawatt meter clearly showed 650 megawatts. Eko Nugroho immediately raised his hand.

"Mr. Dale. Why only 650 megawatts?"

"We had a transmission system issue yesterday that forced us to reduce power into the grid and unit – 1 is still waiting for the grid okay to increase power." A lie, or at least a half-truth. There was no reason to explain xenon transients to a political delegation.

“Mr. Dale. May I ask why transmission issues? You have a very large power plant. Is it too large for the power grid?”

The question caught Dale off guard. It felt cynical, almost pointed.

“We occasionally have line loading issues depending on which other plants are running. Sometimes the grid gets congested.”

“Do you require more power lines?”

Nugroho was obviously savvy. As Dale prepared to answer, the control room radio cracked with an urgent, distorted voice.

“CONTROL ROOM, WE HAVE A HYDRAULIC OIL LEAK AT THE CONTROL VALVES ON THE MAIN TURBINE. IT IS SPRAYING HARD!”

Billy Moss snapped his head toward the turbine panel, grabbed his hardhat, and bounded out the door. Chaos ensued. A loud siren began its wailing ascent. The auxiliary operator's voice jumped an octave as he screamed into the radio.

"CONTROL ROOM! THE LEAK HAS IGNITED! WE HAVE A FIRE UNDER UNIT - 1 TURBINE! I REPEAT, WE HAVE A FIRE UNDER THE TURBINE!"

Billy Moss's voice immediately barked over the air.

"CONTROL ROOM, TRIP THE EHC HYDRAULIC PUMPS ON UNIT 1!"

"TRIPPING UNIT 1 MAIN TURBINE HYDRAULIC PUMPS!" the RO shouted back.

There was a floor-shaking thump as the steam stop and control valves slammed closed, isolating steam to the massive turbine.

"CONFIRMING UNIT 1 HYDRAULIC PUMPS OFF!" the SRO yelled.

"UNIT 1 TURBINE TRIP! UNIT 1 REACTOR SCRAM!"

The room became a symphony of flashing alarms and discordant horns.

"INITIATE SCRAM AND TURBINE TRIP PROTOCOLS!"

The radio barked again. It was Billy Moss. "FIRE IS EXTINGUISHED UNDER THE UNIT 1 TURBINE! FIRE IS EXTINGUISHED!"

"ROGER, CONFIRMING FIRE EXTINGUISHED. SECURING TURBINE FIRE SUPPRESSION SYSTEM!"

"ALL CONTROL RODS DROPPED," the RO called out, his eyes scanning the board. "REACTOR IS SCRAMMED. CONFIRMING MAIN TURBINE IS ROLLING DOWN."

Dale turned to the delegation. They were wild-eyed. Warren Buffton was ashen, and even the normally composed Stephen Langford wore a look of abject fear. He said something into Cal's ear. Cal gritted his teeth and darted over to Dale.

"This was supposed to be a showcase visit," Cal hissed. "What the hell happened?"

Dale winced, stunned by the lawyer's focus, but he kept his voice professional. He raised his arms to the group. "Folks, folks, this is not a nuclear emergency! The steam turbine tripped and shut down the reactor automatically. This is exactly how the safety systems are designed to work. Everything is okay. As soon as I get the all-clear from the CSE, we will move back to the administration building."

The delegation watched anxiously for several more minutes as the operators secured the plant. Finally, Billy Moss returned and guardedly signaled that they could leave.

The coming weeks were a zoo at Torlon Hills. The Nuclear Regulatory Commission appeared almost immediately and began a thorough investigation. Nuclear sins are not easily forgiven nor forgotten by the NRC.

Dale and his Ops Managers spent several days in meetings to satisfy the regulatory agency. Nothing unusual, but grueling nonetheless.

The fire was traced to an incorrect O-ring installed in a high-pressure hydraulic oil line. It was a standard rubber O-ring; it should have been Viton. The industry standard for hydraulic fluid on steam turbines was a product called Fyrquel. It was a phosphate ester-based fluid that was self-extinguishing when exposed to high temperatures. It would dissolve standard rubber products. The material had simply failed under operating conditions.

Their highly experienced warehouse supervisor had retired the previous winter when they put the ADM system into the warehouse for consumable and cost tracking service. An expensive system but ultimately would result in greater savings from better inventory control.

His replacement relied strictly on the ADM documentation, His understanding of the material was limited to what was shown on his display. The error had been signed off by a peer who knew no better. They were both punished accordingly.

They also determined the failure was aided by the power reduction. The massive steam turbine's vibration increased to near alarm point as the load on it was decreased. This was due to known cracks in the rotor. These cracks were being managed and monitored by the engineering group. The rotor had not been repaired or replaced due to budget constraints and the understanding that it would be taken care of in a future outage. Engineering had recommended replacement two years earlier after ultrasonic inspections revealed the first signs of cracking. The estimate had been large. The rotor was massive and the machine work specialized.

At the corporate level the decision had seemed reasonable. The turbine still ran. The monitoring systems showed the cracks were stable. The plant had just come through an expensive refueling outage. Capital spending across the fleet was already under scrutiny. So the recommendation moved quietly into a folder labeled Future

Work. Machines do not read budgets. They only obey physics.

The reactor SCRAM and subsequent shutdown had been flawless. The fire suppression system functioned as intended. There was no radiological release. However, the NRC focused its investigation on material control and maintenance verification processes. Unit 1 remained offline through the remainder of the fuel cycle and into the scheduled refueling outage.

Dale kept his position. Barely. Dale understood the politics of it immediately. Inside a nuclear plant the chain of responsibility always led to the plant manager. It did not matter that the O-ring mistake had occurred in the warehouse, or that the rotor replacement had been deferred by corporate capital planning. When something went wrong, the plant manager owned the result. Dale had believed that principle his entire career. Now he was living inside it.

Cal argued for his removal, but many still highly respected Dale's record and the plant's prior performance. Stephen Langford was deeply embarrassed and took the SCRAM and shutdown personally.

Cal argued that Dale should have been on top of the warehouse failure and faulted him for poor training and for allowing the delegation into the control room knowing they had a vibration issue that could have compromised the visiting delegation.

Dale had little recourse. The captain goes down with the ship. He knew the implications of a situation such as this.

This would not be Dale's final test at MidAtlantic. Not even close.

***

Part 5

Callie McGraw

****

Orville Donovan, the senior meteorologist at the weather prediction center in College Park, Maryland, sat nervously staring at the Atlantic sector for the entire afternoon. He was sometimes called “The Prophet” by his coworkers.

He switched to the upper-air charts. The jet stream over the eastern United States was beginning to buckle southward, forming a deeper trough than the models had shown just two days earlier.

He tapped the screen lightly with his pencil, as if it might change something.

“That’s farther south than it should be.”

He frequently spoke out loud to himself when studying weather patterns. Cold air was already draining down from central Canada. The temperature anomalies were modest for now, but the trajectory was unmistakable.

The air mass was sliding toward New England and the Mid-Atlantic instead of remaining bottled up over the Great Lakes.

He pulled up the ensemble runs. The individual simulations were still scattered, but their average was slowly shifting in the same direction but slightly colder and slightly wetter. Each new run nudged the track of a potential coastal low a little farther west. It was not proof of anything, just a trend. He leaned back uncomfortably in his chair, shaking his head.

When patterns like this began locking together, a blocking high over Greenland, a deepening eastern trough, cold air draining south… Storms along the Atlantic seaboard had a habit of slowing down and reorganizing in unpleasant ways. He had seen it before.

The models were still days away from agreeing on anything specific, but the ingredients were assembling in a way he didn't like. He studied the screen for another moment.

"Something's coming," he murmured.

He rubbed his right ear and shook his head slowly.

"I've seen this pattern before. It usually ends badly."

***

Sentinel Creek Generating Station entered Warren Buffton's MidAtlantic empire almost by accident. It came bundled with the much larger and strategically indispensable High Mesa Energy Center during an acquisition that most analysts focused on for entirely different reasons. High Mesa was the prize. Sentinel Creek was the paperwork.

The plant manager, Callie McGraw, understood that better than anyone. It was a modest 1 × 1 combined cycle built around a GE Frame 7E, commissioned when rotary phones were still common in control rooms. One industrial gas turbine. One heat recovery steam generator. One small steam turbine. On a good day it could produce about 120 megawatts. Not enough to impress analysts. Just enough to matter when things went wrong.

To the money gurus orbiting Warren's financial universe, Sentinel Creek was a rounding error. A maintenance expense. An inconvenience. What the spreadsheets could not capture was how electrical systems actually behaved under stress. Grids did not fail politely or in tidy increments. When the wrong pieces disappeared at the wrong moment, entire regions could go dark with startling speed.

Sentinel Creek was one of only two black start facilities in the entire MidAtlantic fleet. If the unthinkable happened, this plant would be the first spark in the dark. Sentinel Creek did not look like the sort of place that guarded the beginning of civilization.

Most mornings Callie walked the plant before going into her office. The habit had started when she was a young engineer and had never left her. Operators joked that she trusted steel and valves more than reports.

The Frame 7E sat low and squat inside the turbine hall, its casing stained by decades of heat cycles. The HRSG structure rose behind it like an industrial cathedral of pipes and catwalks. Everything about the station felt slightly undersized compared to the giant combined cycles spreading across the country. But small plants had advantages.

Callie stopped briefly beside the diesel building and rested her hand on the vibration-dampened wall. Inside, the two black-start engines waited in silence.

If the grid ever collapsed, these machines would be among the first to speak. Most people in MidAtlantic had forgotten that. Callie McGraw had not.

Large power plants cannot start themselves. When they go completely dark, electricity must come from somewhere else to bring them back to life. Once running, they can produce enormous amounts of electricity. On the backside of the plant, behind the aging 7E at Sentinel Creek sat two faithfully maintained 12-megawatt diesel generators.

In a separate annex, humming with the kind of vibration that loosened dental work, lived a 23-megawatt LM-2500 aero-derivative gas turbine. It looked as though it had crossed the Atlantic on the Mayflower and had never forgiven anyone for it. You needed a tetanus shot just to look at it.

The probability of a full grid collapse was small enough that financial planners ignored it. Sentinel Creek had been built by people who did not ignore such things. Unfortunately, those people were now long gone.

The only constant at Sentinel Creek for nearly two decades was Callie McGraw. "Bulldog," the corporate engineers called her. It was meant as a compliment.

Callie fought her way into this world before she ever understood what the word meant. Twenty-three weeks into pregnancy, her mother's car was broadsided by a drunk driver. Her injuries were severe.

Callie was delivered by emergency Cesarean section in the hospital emergency room a few hours later. Her dad, Dean, drove at breakneck speed to the hospital when he received word of the accident. He did not have to wait long before he got the news.

Outside the operating suite, a surgeon stepped into the hallway and addressed the tall, weathered man waiting there.

“Dean McGraw?”

“That would be me,” he said quietly, the desperation in his eyes impossible to ignore.

“Your wife is conscious and doing well despite a broken hip, femur, and several broken ribs.”

Dean nodded quickly.

“What about the baby?”

The surgeon paused.

“Your baby girl was delivered by Cesarean a few minutes ago. We estimate she is at twenty-three to twenty-four weeks development.”

He hesitated only briefly.

"She is in the neonatal intensive care unit. At this point her chances are about fifty-fifty. The next twenty-four hours will be critical."

Dean swallowed hard. The surgeon gave him a faint smile.

"We have one of the best NICU teams in the country. She's in good hands."

He turned to go back into the emergency room, then paused.

"Your little girl is a fighter. She made sure we knew she didn't approve of arriving early."

Dean's eyes watered. The lump in his throat got larger.

"Sophie and I have been trying a long time to have a child."

The surgeon nodded sympathetically.

"Your wife began hemorrhaging during the accident. While we were able to save your daughter, your wife will not be able to have more children."

They named their little fighter, Callie. It was a family name from Dean's Irish side. His great-great-grandmother survived the Irish famine. Family stories said she saved several relatives from starvation.

Callie inherited the dark complexion of her Latina mother rather than the fair skin of her Irish father. She struggled in school. Not because she failed to understand the material, but because reading itself seemed to fight her at every step. Words reversed themselves. Letters drifted across the page as if they refused to stay put. Symbols blurred into shapes that made no sense.

She cried at home in the evenings because she could not understand what was on the page, yet somehow she already knew the answers.

In middle school a perceptive teacher noticed something unusual. Callie excelled in mathematics yet frequently confused simple operators. The symbols for "greater than" and "less than" often seemed meaningless to her. The school arranged testing.

A few days later Callie came home to find her parents waiting in the front room. Her father spoke first with his usual blunt honesty.

"Callie, we got the results of those tests you took. Turns out you're not dumb. Just confused."

"Dean!" Sophie snapped immediately, glaring at him.

She knelt beside Callie.

"Honey, the tests say you have something called dyslexia. It makes reading harder for you. But they say they can help with it."

Dean nodded vigorously.

"They also said you're smart. Like, really smart. You just need help with your… dis-lexical thing."

He frowned slightly.

"Whatever they called it."

Callie began working with Karen Spars, a dyslexia specialist at school. Karen quickly discovered something unusual. Callie wasn't just determined. She was relentless. Using unconventional teaching methods, Callie's world opened up as it had never before.

At home, Sophie McGraw ran a daycare to help support the family. She believed all children mattered. Her "kids" were blessed to have Sophie McGraw in their lives.

Her dad, Dean, regularly drove freight across three states, his stubborn Irish pride matched only by a back brace that creaked louder than his truck. He was gone more often than he was home. In his mind, his primary duty was to financially take care of his family. Everything else was secondary. Sophie was the one who made everything work.

Dean and Sophie impressed two simple rules on Callie. Work hard. Never surrender.

Early in middle school, Callie learned something else: other people's opinions did not define her. It was the first time she became aware that her dark skin tone had different effects on some people. At first she cried alone in her bedroom in the evenings. She then realized with the help of her mother that other kids could be mean, but it didn't change who she was. The crying ended.

Dyslexia dragged her grades just low enough to keep most academic awards out of reach. Scholarships were scarce. Didn't matter. She had an unquenchable desire to learn.

Engineering school came through a patchwork of smaller scholarships she hunted down herself and student loans she signed without hesitation. Fast-food dinners and black coffee were not indulgences. They were daily sustenance.

She earned a mechanical engineering degree from the New Jersey Institute of Technology. It wasn't Ivy League, but it was affordable. She never apologized for it and she never needed to.

Callie first arrived at Sentinel Creek as a summer intern. The plant was still young then. The steel still bright.

The Frame 7E carried itself with restrained promise. She fell in love with the symmetry of it all. The steam lines, the turbines, the clean mechanical logic of turning heat into electricity.

After graduation she returned as a temporary engineer overseeing installation of the two 12-megawatt black-start diesel generators. She memorized the bid specifications. Torque values lived in her head. She questioned weld procedures that drifted even slightly from code.

Though trained mechanically, she gravitated toward the electrical systems that tied everything together. During construction the site foreman misjudged her badly. He was replaced within a week. No one tested her boundaries again.

The diesels met specifications in full. Young Callie made certain of it. She was hired as a full-time staff engineer shortly afterward. Corporate engineers soon learned her name. When numbers refused to reconcile and drawings refused to cooperate, someone inevitably said the same thing:

"Call Callie."

The nickname "Bulldog" stuck.

She never objected to it. Years passed. Managers rotated through Sentinel Creek in revolving-door fashion. Callie remained, steadfast, a stalwart of Sentinel Creek Generating Station. Her sometimes-blunt demeanor was seen negatively by many of the men she worked around. Power plants are often men's clubs that tend to exclude women. Callie was aware of this. She was also aware that she studied relentlessly and understood the plant as well or better than anyone she worked with at Sentinel Creek.

As she matured, her dyslexia began working in her favor. She naturally viewed systems holistically instead of focusing on isolated details. That instinct later helped her understand both plant operations and the electrical grid.

She always remembered back to her first realization that her skin was darker than most of her friends during her final years of elementary school. She remembered crying in her room. She also remembered how beautiful her mother was, and that most people seemed struck by her beauty. She didn't see herself as pretty, but she knew she looked like her mother, and everyone always commented on her mother's attractiveness.

Each subsequent plant manager tended to lean on her plant understanding more than the previous. While she felt these managers were running the plant vicariously through her, she kept silent and did everything they asked with good attitude.

On more than one occasion her understanding of the plant and quick thinking saved the current plant manager embarrassment, or worse. Yet, when they moved on, Callie was overlooked for the promotion. Other plant manager positions opened in the MidAtlantic system. She would make her interest known but was never even given an interview. Still, her attitude survived these little rejections, and she strove harder to improve her understanding, especially on the electrical side of the plant. She often felt that if she had it to do over again, she would have sought a degree in electrical engineering and not mechanical. Not that she didn't care for the mechanical side, but the electrical side intrigued her, and she seemed to grasp it in an organic way that she couldn't explain. It just came naturally to her.

Her promotion finally came through attrition and quiet competence. Eventually her title caught up with the work she had already been doing.

Plant Manager.

Her two-year marriage to Russell Pike ended quickly, painfully. Callie fell in love with him knowing he had a temper. Her father had a temper too, but he had always been a good man. Russell was not. The first time he struck her it was over a dropped coffee mug. She insisted on counseling. She made it clear that if he ever hit her again the marriage would end. A year later it did. Callie returned to her maiden name and closed that chapter of her life. To reduce the pain of her failed marriage, she focused on the electrical backbone of the fleet. Callie became an ardent student of grid dynamics and restart procedures. Transmission planners and plant managers across the system began calling her when questions about system recovery surfaced. Over time she became the quiet architect of MidAtlantic's black-start strategy.

She mapped restart sequences across the grid that many executives considered theoretical and unnecessary. Callie disagreed. The grid was not theoretical. Years of wrestling with dyslexia had trained her mind to see systems differently. Patterns appeared where others saw complexity.

When MidAtlantic imposed sweeping budget cuts, Sentinel Creek barely noticed. You cannot take away what was never granted. Callie made it work. She knew if she complained it would be held against her. Therefore, she learned to budget extremely carefully, and always kept contingency plans in her mind.

While working with Joel Adamson's group on black start initiatives, she was able to visit a few of the other plants and different areas of the transmission system. They were always cordial to her but never wanted to engage in deep technical discussions. She thought it had something to do with her. Later she realized it was probably insecurity on their part.

On one of her system visits she finally met Dale Morrison. Despite the recent shutdown that had played out poorly in front of Warren Buffton and his circle, Dale Morrison remained the standard by which plant managers were measured. His was the largest station in the fleet. It was nuclear. She managed the smallest and oldest plant in the system. Dale had more janitors at Torlon Hills than she had employees.

It took her over an hour to clear security and reach his administrative wing. She had not scheduled the meeting; he agreed to give her a few quick minutes.

His office was large but orderly, walls lined with awards earned by Torlon Hills since its inception, including the Power Magazine plant of the year, twice.

Dale stood and greeted her when she entered.

"So," he said evenly, "are you the Callie McGraw who's been rewriting our black start assumptions?"

Her answer came before caution could intercept it.

"Depends. Am I being evaluated or thanked?"

A pause. Then the faintest smile at the corner of his mouth.

"Neither. I've read your analysis. It's brilliant and thorough."

She studied him before sitting. He was not dismissive. Not distracted. He was actually listening.

"Most of the fleet thinks black start is academic," she said dryly. "It isn't."

"I fully agree."

The simplicity of that answer unsettled her more than opposition would have.

"Do you know Kendall Allen?" he asked.

"Only in passing."

He hesitated, a rare event.

"I'm not convinced he's prioritizing the right risks."

She did not smile. She did not need to. Their eyes locked together and communicated the truth.

They talked for more than forty-five minutes. Transmission bottlenecks, VAR support limitations, islanding strategies, and switching orders that existed only in theory. He followed her reasoning intently without interruption. When she paused, he waited.

At one point he asked, "What would you change if you could change anything?"

No one had asked her that before. Prior to this she fought for any perceived victories.

"The procedure assumes a cooperative grid," she said intently. "We don't have one. If multiple corridors are unavailable, we won't carry initial load. We need predefined islands. Actual switching orders. Not conference slides."

Dale did not answer immediately.

He turned slightly in his chair and looked through the office window toward the distant cooling towers. Even from here they dominated the skyline above the river valley. Twenty-six hundred megawatts of nuclear generation rested behind those concrete walls.

"What you're describing," he said slowly, "is a restart procedure designed for a damaged grid, not a healthy one."

"Yes."

He folded his hands on the desk.

"That assumption will make people uncomfortable."

Callie shrugged faintly.

"The grid doesn't care about comfort."

For the first time since she entered the room, Dale laughed quietly.

"Good," he said. "Neither do I."

He leaned back, nodding his head slowly, considering her words carefully.

“We were forced to fifty percent load twice this quarter because of transmission bottlenecks,” he said. “Cycling a nuclear unit to satisfy line constraints isn’t sustainable nor efficient.”

Their eyes again held a moment longer than required. He didn’t look away first.

She noticed.

He was sophisticated, complex, and unmistakably attractive.

They agreed to collaborate quietly on revising the black start framework. He gave her his personal cell number. He told himself it was strictly for business. He hoped that wasn’t entirely true.

“Call anytime,” he said. “This one matters. Maybe more than most would admit.”

When she left Torlon Hills, she understood two things.

The grid was far more fragile than anyone in corporate believed. For the first time in years, she had found someone else who understood what might happen if the lights ever went out.

***

Part 6

Equipment Decay

****

Eric Glanville sat in front of the large control console at Blackstone Generating Station. He had dimmed the control room lights earlier as his eyes were bothering him. 2:35 in the morning and he should be asleep like the rest of "normal" society.

His head bobbed unevenly as he nodded off to sleep. He had now worked rotating shift work for eight long years, despising every moment of it. Unfortunately, it was the best job he ever had.

Spending a good part of the day assembling his son's jungle gym in the backyard didn't help. Two hours of sleep was not enough to exist on, let alone run a 500 megawatt combined cycle plant.

Shift turnover was routine. Feedwater pump – A outboard motor bearing was still running hot. Nothing new there. Main fuel gas pressure into the plant was unsteady. Nothing new there.

At Blackstone, gas pressure was rarely steady like the other plants. Blackstone was on the southern side of the MidAtlantic system and purchased its gas from Kandor-Martin Gas Company. It was the only plant in the MidAtlantic to do so. Gas pressure was always unpredictable, especially in the heavy use periods in the winter.

He slipped off to sleep again only to be awakened by an alarm horn. His head snapped upwards to the large overhead alarm display and he squinted, trying to focus on the latest alarm.

0337 – MN FUEL GAS PRESSURE LOW – 499 PSIG

His heart skipped a beat. He acknowledged the alarm and sat up in the chair. While the main gas pressure frequently drifted, it rarely went into low alarm. Two minutes later the alarm horn sounded again.

0339 – MN FUEL GAS PRESSURE LOW LOW – 490 PSIG

His heart rate increased dramatically as he acknowledged the alarm. At 485 psig the gas turbines would trip offline. He didn't want to deal with a unit trip. Not tonight. Not ever. Three minutes later the LOW LOW alarm cleared. A minute later the LOW alarm cleared.

There was no call from Kandor-Martin gas company. This was not normal.

***

Silver Ridge Energy Center had begun experiencing an uptick in operational failures. Nothing catastrophic. Not yet.

At Silver Ridge Block 1, the steam turbine suffered a thrust-bearing failure at rated load. The unit shut down immediately. The maintenance superintendent told management six months, best case. Specialized machine work and long-lead parts would determine the final schedule.

Silver Ridge was not alone. Franklin Energy Center and several other MidAtlantic stations had also begun experiencing similar problems. Morale across several plants had eroded. Turnover was rising. Maintenance intervals were quietly stretching.

Franklin held particular importance. It was the second black-start facility in the MidAtlantic fleet. Sentinel Creek anchored the southwest. Franklin protected the north. Most of the generation and major load centers lay between them.

When MidAtlantic acquired Franklin, it inherited an aging Pratt & Whitney FT-4 Twin-Pac. Two early-1960s, Boeing 707-era engines fed hot exhaust into separate power turbines, and the turbines drove a single generator through reduction gears.

It was a strange machine, half aviation relic, half emergency equipment. Loud, temperamental, and spectacularly inefficient.

The unit had been relocated years earlier from the retired Remy Glen coal station because it required almost no new capital. Since it already existed and still ran, it was the perfect corporate solution.

As a black-start unit, efficiency did not matter. It was expected to operate rarely, briefly, and under controlled conditions. Out of sight. Out of mind.

Callie had just finished a performance review for one of her operators when her phone rang.

"Callie McGraw speaking."

"Callie, it's Dale Morrison."

His tone was unusually direct.

"I've come across something interesting," he said. "And I know I can trust you with it."

She waited.

"I have reason to believe Franklin hasn't been testing their black-start unit."

Callie sat up slightly.

"Why?"

"Nepotism," Dale said with a quiet sigh. "I've got a cousin working there. Honestly, he's not very bright."

A brief pause.

"Wrong side of the family."

Callie smiled despite herself.

"Do you have a plan?"

"I just executed it," he said. "I told you."

He exhaled and smiled.

"I've got a refueling outage going sideways and a pile of regulatory issues stacked on my desk. You didn't hear this from me."

The lack of testing bothered her immediately.

The fact that Dale had called her bothered her differently.

She had accumulated substantial PTO over the years and rarely used it. Within the hour she decided to visit her parents.

They lived in Millstone Junction, conveniently positioned between Silver Ridge and Franklin. Torlon Hills lay roughly 120 miles southeast of Franklin.

The drive took seven hours. She hated every mile. Flying was not much better. Door-to-door it often took five hours trying to navigate Sentinel Creek's regional airport delays and mandatory layovers in Cincinnati or Charlotte. Driving was usually faster.

Her parents welcomed her warmly. They were aging gracefully and seemed to appreciate her visits more with each passing year. As an only child, she dominated their attention. Usually more than she was comfortable with.

The familiar questions surfaced quickly.

"Are you seeing anyone?"

"Will we ever see grandchildren?"

Callie smiled and deflected as she always did.

The next morning she called Teddy Warnick, the plant manager at Franklin, and asked if she could stop by while she was in the area. He hesitated, but lacked a good reason to refuse. After hanging up she debated calling Dale. Her distraction did not go unnoticed.

"Everything okay?" her mother asked.

"Just work," Callie said.

She finally dialed Dale's number.

"I'm at my parents' place in Millstone Junction. Teddy gave me permission to visit Franklin."

A pause.

"Your secret's safe, but I want to see what's happening up there."

"I'm impressed," Dale said. "I'd give my left arm to go with you, but this outage isn't cooperating."

His voice lowered.

"Franklin's sliding. Teddy blames the budget. Corporate blames Teddy."

A familiar pattern.

“Callie,” he said quietly, “I want to know what you find.”

Franklin looked tired before anyone said a word. The paint on several handrails had gone chalky. Small weeds pushed through cracks along the parking lot. Nothing dramatic. Nothing that would alarm a visiting executive. But enough small signs had accumulated to suggest the same thing Callie had seen at other drifting plants. Standards were no longer leading behavior. Circumstances were.

Security was minimal. She called the control room from the gate phone and was waved through.

Eric Royden, the maintenance manager, met her near an empty reception desk and led her toward his office.

“Visiting a power plant on your day off?” he asked with a crooked smile. “You a glutton for punishment?”

Callie laughed.

“Something like that.”

She let the conversation drift casually before asking her question.

"Who maintains your black-start Twin-Pac?"

Eric glanced at his computer screen.

"Alex Cordon handles it."

And just like that, she was handed off.

Alex met her with easy conversation and led her toward the far eastern corner of the plant.

The Twin-Pac enclosure sat near the perimeter fence, painted a fading oxidized green. A large silver maple nearby had spent years anointing it with a blanket of leaves and small branches. At first glance it appeared to be an abandoned relic.

They climbed onto the small golf cart. He immediately noticed her faint perfume. It energized him. He became noticeably more attentive than he had been in the office.

Callie used the moment.

"When was the last time this unit was started?"

Alex shrugged.

"No idea. I'm an ICE tech, not an operator. You'd have to ask Mike Cummings."

"Who maintains it?"

Alex laughed.

"You assume it's maintained."

Arriving at the Twin-Pac, he wrestled open an enclosure door on the number-one engine. It broke loose with a metallic shriek. The smell of fuel oil immediately drifted out. Not a good sign.

"It still uses the original electromechanical relays and ladder logic," Alex said. "We told management it should be upgraded to digital controls, but the cost was too high."

He watched her reaction carefully.

"Last time I worked on it I spent hours tracking down a bad Agastat timer relay. Took two days to find a replacement."

Callie circled the unit slowly. One detail caught her eye immediately. The exhaust stack drain valve on the number-one engine was closed.

"Alex, this has to stay open," she said.

He looked over.

"If rainwater fills that exhaust chamber and someone tries to start this engine, it can do real damage."

Alex shrugged defensively.

"Not my job. I fix things when they break. That's Mike Cummings' territory."

Callie moved to the generator enclosure and forced open another sticky inspection panel. Between the generator base and the enclosure wall lay a row of stained sorbent oil booms. Shop towels surrounded a slow, persistent drip from the shaft seals. She crouched and pressed one lightly. The boom compressed easily. It was old and saturated.

It was obvious what had happened. Someone had learned how to live with the leak, but no one had fixed it. Alex saw the look of concern on Callie's face.

"They've always leaked," Alex said. "Sixty-year-old machine."

She stood and pointed toward oil running along the cracked concrete foundation.

"Where does that drain?"

Alex pointed toward a shallow, hand-dug trench along the slab.

"It eventually reaches the yard separator."

She nodded once. At Sentinel Creek one of her operators would have been written up for that.

Back in the admin building Alex introduced her to Mike Cummings. He appeared irritated before she even spoke.

"We test that damn thing every month," he said. "Sometimes it starts. Sometimes it doesn't. We've had a control upgrade in the budget three years running. It never gets approved."

Callie nodded. She already knew the budget story.

"When you test it," she asked carefully, "do you synchronize and load it, or just bring it to speed?"

Mike's minimal patience evaporated.

"Callie, we've got emergency diesels on both generation blocks. We test them under load every month. The batteries keep the control systems alive, the diesels keep the batteries charged."

He leaned forward.

"We can shut this plant down safely all day long."

Callie's Irish Latina temper flared momentarily and then settled into something colder.

"Mike," she said as evenly as she could, "shutting down isn't the issue."

She met his eyes.

"Starting back up is."

He said nothing.

“The Twin-Pac isn’t there to shut you down,” she continued. “It’s there to start you back up.”

Silence hung between them.

“Once Franklin is online again,” she said, “you can energize Silver Ridge. Cannon Creek. Pine Grove.”

She paused.

“The Twin-Pac isn’t critical to Franklin.”

“It’s critical to the grid.”

Mike leaned back with a tired shake of his head.

“Maybe you should convince Kendall Allen to fund it.”

Callie pressed one final question.

“When was the last time it synchronized to the grid and carried load?”

Mike shrugged.

“It’s been a while.”

Back in the parking lot she called Dale. He didn’t answer.

A text arrived moments later.

In meeting.

Dinner?

That diner on Main Street, Millstone Junction. 7:00.

She stared at the screen longer than necessary. Surprised. Curious. Unsure. After several minutes, she sent a thumbs-up emoji. The rest of the drive back to her folks she wondered if the emoji had been a mistake.

Back in Millstone Junction, she hugged her mother quickly.

"Can't have dinner here tonight. I have some business to attend."

She hesitated, then lowered her voice.

"Can I borrow some makeup?"

The diner's neon sign buzzed faintly in the dusk. A white MidAtlantic pickup sat in the busy parking lot. A company vehicle. This meant official business. Good.

Dale stood when she approached the table and extended his hand.

"So. How are you doing?" He asked with a warm smile.

"Good. It was…" She paused and raised her eyebrows. "An interesting day."

The dinner rush filled the room with clatter and conversation. It gave them cover. She spoke first, walking him through the Twin-Pac debacle. The leaks, the attitudes, the slow erosion of standards. He listened without interrupting.

When she finished, he leaned forward slightly.

"Do you have a plan?"

She smiled.

"I just executed it. I told you."

He caught the reference. They both laughed.

They talked until the diner closed at ten that night. Most of it was business. Black start sequencing. Switching constraints. Assumptions no one had verified in years. Toward the end of the evening the conversation drifted. Where they grew up. Family. Education. Small disclosures.

Nothing dramatic. Both enjoyed it more than they intended to.

Since his divorce, Dale had buried himself inside Torlon Hills. It was easier to think about megawatts than silence. Easier to manage workforce and reactor physics than personal memory. He did not talk about Carla. At one point he just lowered his head slightly and quietly told her that he was divorced.

With little forethought Callie said, “I was married for two years to a man that had serious anger issues. It turned physical and I could not manage it any longer.”

“I’m sorry.” Dale said with sincerity in his voice. Their pain passed silently between them.

Outside, the night air had cooled. He walked her to her car.

“When are you heading back to Sentinel Creek?”

“Probably the day after tomorrow. I still have a lot of PTO to burn.”

He opened her door. As she settled into the seat, he hesitated and then said it.

“Would you like the VIP tour of a large nuclear plant before you go?”

A flicker of excitement crossed her face before she could stop it.

“That would be nice. Do you know anyone who can provide a tour without, like, serious drama?”

They both laughed.

“Tomorrow? Around noon?”

“That works.”

He closed the door gently.

“I’ll see you there.”

Callie arrived at Torlon Hills just before noon the next day. Security was expecting her. She was whisked through the admin building directly to Dale’s office.

“It’s good to see you,” Dale said. “I had a nice time last night.”

“So did I.” She paused. “Thanks for the bridge through security. I felt like royalty.”

“I told you it was a VIP tour. My VIPs don’t get hassled by security.” She smiled.

He took her first to the massive maintenance shop.

“This is probably a bit larger than Sentinel Creek’s.” He said with a grin.

“Dale, your office is larger than the maintenance shop at Sentinel Creek.”

They both laughed.

Next stop was the simulator. He had arranged a break in the on-going training. As they entered, he leaned into the instructor’s area where the simulator was controlled.

“Lee, give me a full-power snapshot and cut it loose.”

Switches clicked. The simulator initialized at full power.

"It's all yours," Dale said as he extended his hand into the control area.

"If you've ever wondered what happens when you do something in a nuclear plant, here's your chance."

She didn't miss her chance.

"How fast can you do a load reduction?"

"As fast as we need to. But the faster we move, the more issues we invite. It depends on the fuel cycle, xenon, a dozen other things."

"Can you simulate a rapid grid frequency increase? A transmission line trip where you're suddenly over-generating?" She paused. "Where the turbine tries to overspeed?"

He grinned. "You don't waste any time, do you?"

He picked up the blue phone.

"Lee, give me a transmission trip with a big frequency bump. Not enough to trip us… Just a good hit."

There was a brief delay. Dale watched the turbine controls. Alarms erupted. The megawatt meter fell from

1200 to 600 in seconds. Trend lines went jagged. The room filled with layered sirens.

Callie didn't blink.

"Dale, in less than a second you just shed four times what Sentinel produces at full load."

A few moments later, more alarms flashed. Another siren cut through the noise. Dale looked at her over his glasses.

"The reactor scrammed. Fortunately, the turbine moves almost instantly. Unfortunately, the reactor doesn't. That mismatch will get you every time."

Callie thoughtfully processed what she was seeing.

"Dale, I know how much start-up power it takes to bring the coal plants, and most of the combined cycle plants back up, but how much does it take on a 1200 megawatt nuclear plant?"

He smiled broadly.

"Excellent question. We take about 100 megawatts." He paused. "This includes the surge. When we close the breaker to start one of our reactor feed pumps, there is a surge to get it up to speed that is 6 to 8 times greater than its running current."

She shook her head in agreement. She was very aware of current surges when energizing equipment.

"We can do it with less than 100 megawatts, but it would be iffy."

Like teens on a date, they ran several more scenarios together. After the last one, Callie turned to him.

"This is extraordinary. On the gas plant side, we hire someone and let them shadow an experienced operator. They absorb what they can and we hope it's enough. Formal training barely exists."

Dale's expression shifted.

"It's that age-old argument. You know the one, we can't afford to train." He held her gaze. "The truth is, we can't afford not to train but too many people don't see this."

She nodded in agreement. Her VIP tour continued onto the turbine deck. The massive steam turbines filled the turbine hall, casting long shadows across the floor. From there, they entered the control room.

The tour lasted over three hours. It felt like minutes to Callie. Dale personally walked her through security back to her car in the parking lot. He opened her door and looked into her eyes.

"I hope you don't mind me saying that I think you are an extraordinary lady."

Her face flushed. She hadn't experienced emotion like this in many years.

"Thanks. I think you are pretty amazing yourself." She looked back at the plant for a moment. "I can't tell you how much I appreciate the time you spent with me today. It was incredibly interesting."

She got into the car. He leaned in.

"I would like to see you again. If you can see your way clear to use a few more days of PTO, we could make a pilgrimage to the MARES Systems Operation Control center outside of Allentown."

Concern crossed her face.

"What about your refueling outage, and the issues at the plant?"

He flushed this time.

"I haven't taken any time off in months. This place won't crumble in a day."

"Yeah, I would love to. It is another piece of the puzzle that I would certainly like to see."

She paused and fortified her resolve.

"Yes, absolutely, let's do it."

***

Part 7

SOC

****

Jerry Evans knocked gently on Orville Donovan's door frame at the weather prediction center in College Park, Maryland. Orville looked up from the trio of displays he was diligently studying.

"Can I help you?" Orville asked politely. Jerry was his immediate supervisor. Orville felt he was a good supervisor, but he lacked the instinct that had earned Orville the nickname 'the Prophet.'

"Orville, I just read your most recent report. Do I understand it correctly? You are emphatically warning that we are headed for a severe weather event that the computer models are not yet indicating as such?"

"I am."

He looked away from Jerry and focused on his left display.

“The temperature anomalies are modest right now, but the trajectory is off. Not a lot, but it just doesn’t feel right. The air mass is sliding toward New England and the Mid-Atlantic instead of remaining bottled up over the Great Lakes.”

He sighed loudly, rubbed his ear, and continued.

“Jerry, I know you like sticking with the computer models, and I know they are usually accurate, but something doesn’t feel right. The pattern is off. I sense patterns and this pattern is bothering me.”

Jerry watched Orville rub his right ear. He knew this was a nervous tick of his. He had seen it for years.

“Orville, we have over five hundred million dollars of analytical computer modeling hardware and software forecasting an unremarkable winter storm and you want me to go to my superiors and sound the alarm that the software is wrong, and you think that this is far more than a normal winter storm?”

Orville looked up at Jerry and flatly said, “I do. I think the software is seriously understating the event.”

“You do realize the position this puts me in, don’t you?”

Orville stared back at his displays.

“Jerry, you do what you must do, I am telling you that what I am seeing is not good.”

***

Dale picked up Callie at exactly 7:00 AM the next morning.

The drive to the System Operations Center took a little over two hours. By the time they reached the interstate they had already worked their way through politics, religion, and the uneasy state of the country. They discovered they agreed on almost everything.

They both had deep Christian convictions, though they were not evangelical about them. Their comfort level for each other grew continuously. Dale had not allowed anyone to get this close to him in years, not since before

Carla left. Callie stopped letting her guard down years earlier. But her normally impenetrable shield was slowly being dismantled by this man.

About thirty minutes prior to arriving at the System Operations Center Dale made a quick glance at Callie.

"I would ask if you have questions about the SOC but you have probably already done your homework."

Callie nodded slowly.

"I can sum it up quickly. Please correct any errors in understanding." She smiled.

"All of the regional system operations centers across the continent are funded by the utilities with tariffs assessed by their electrical production. They are considered non profit organizations, and the tariffs pay for the infrastructure and labor." She stopped and looked at him inquisitively. "Correct?"

"That is accurate."

"The SOC, in our case MARES, monitors and controls power flows, VARs, voltages, and dispatches the generation to meet load requirements for all the plants in their service area. They also dictate and manage the development of black start capabilities and procedures to the power producers in their pools." She looked over at him again. "Still accurate?"

"Yup."

She reached the limit of her understanding. She then asked, "How is their management group selected?"

Dale kept his eyes on the road.

"I guess you would have to say, they are technically independent."

She waited.

"The Board comes through a stakeholder process. Generators, transmission owners, load-serving entities, marketers. A nomination committee filters candidates, then sector-weighted ballots decide."

"And then?"

"Generation gets the same voting strength as transmission. Transmission gets the same as load. It's balanced. In theory."

"In theory?" she echoed.

"They're required to have no financial interest in any market participant. No stock ownership above a threshold. No active employment in the industry."

"That sounds clean."

"It sounds clean" he agreed reluctantly.

She looked closely at him.

"And in practice?"

"In practice, most of them come from finance, regulatory law, or prior executive roles. Very few have operated a power plant. Fewer have ever sat in a control room during a frequency event, or any other upset for that matter."

She absorbed every word.

"They govern reliability standards they've never lived?"

He nodded once.

"They govern the markets," he corrected gently. "Reliability comes through NERC and FERC. But market incentives drive behavior. Reliability rides in the back seat."

"So, if we aren't doing our part in any area such as black start, how do they know?"

Dale caught a glimpse of a state patrolman sitting on the shoulder and quickly adjusted the cruise control before answering.

"They know because we tell them."

She waited.

"Every black start unit provides annual capability documentation. I know you are aware of this because you have had to do it several times at Sentinel Creek. That's when you give them all your reports, test results, restoration time estimates, fuel assurances, station service configurations. They take all of this and model it."

"Model it?" She repeated questioningly.

"They run system restoration simulations based on what we submit. If the paperwork says the unit can start in ninety minutes, they assume it can start in ninety minutes."

"And if it can't?"

He gave a small shrug.

"Then the model is wrong."

"That seems… Optimistic?"

"It's compliance-based," he said. "They audit the documentation. They don't stand next to the unit during a 2 a.m. cold start in freezing rain."

She raised her eyebrows and stared forward.

"So, unless something fails during a scheduled test?"

"They assume it works."

"And if the test is clean on paper?"

"Then it works," he said.

They went silent. The exit for the SOC was coming up.

The SOC security doors opened without ceremony. Callie stepped through first, expecting noise. Instead, she found quiet. Not silence. Never silence. There was the low, constant ventilation hum of a building designed to never lose power. The faint whisper of conditioned air moving through raised flooring. The distant, irregular chirp of alarm tones, brief, acknowledged, extinguished. The sound of keyboards. Nothing frantic. The faint electrical smell settled in her memory.

The room was vast. Tiered rows of operator consoles descended toward a wall that was less a wall than a continent of light. Transmission lines spread across it in patient geometry. Colored flows pulsed along corridors of steel that stretched from one end of the region to the other. Wind output scrolled in the upper left corner. Load curves arced and bent in the upper right. Weather hovered offshore in muted greens and yellows, rotating slowly, as if undecided.

MARES. Mid-Atlantic Regional Energy System.

She had seen the acronym hundreds of times in reports, compliance filings, and countless emails that arrived at Sentinel Creek hours after the fact. She realized this was where many of those emails were born.

Each console held six, sometimes eight displays. One screen carried the full regional one-line. Another zoomed into constrained interfaces. A third tracked interchange schedules with neighboring authorities. Frequency 59.98… 60.01… floated continuously in a small box near the corner of several screens, the wary eyes of the dispatchers always watching this harbinger of issues.

No one was talking loudly. A dispatcher leaned slightly forward, hand on a mouse, adjusting generation setpoints in increments so small they would have been invisible at the plant. A reliability coordinator stood behind another station, arms folded, studying a voltage profile that only she seemed to find interesting.

Dale did not narrate. He let her take it in. Callie realized, after a moment, that no one here touched steel. No one smelled fuel oil or felt the heat of steam leaks. No one heard bearings complain. Yet the entire grid moved at their fingertips.

A thin amber line flickered briefly on the western interface, an oscillation warning. Not red. Not yet. It blinked twice and settled back to green. No one in the room reacted, but one operator's eyes shifted. Just slightly. A hand hovered over the keyboard a fraction longer than necessary before typing three quiet commands. Somewhere, a gas turbine ramped upward 10 megawatts. Somewhere else, a tie schedule eased by the same amount.

The frequency box trembled.

59.97.

Then 59.99.

Then 60.00.

The room never reacted. It adjusted. For a brief moment Callie imagined what the room would look like if the correction did not come.

Not a dramatic collapse. Nothing cinematic. Just the numbers drifting the wrong direction.

59.85.

59.75.

The operators would still look calm. The adjustments would still be small. A few more megawatts here. A tie-line eased there. Someone would pick up a phone and speak in the same measured voice.

Only later would the alarms begin to layer together. Frequency. Voltage. Interface limits. Protection systems acting faster than the people watching them.

She had seen what machines did when protection ran out of margin. Turbines did not politely slow down. Generators did not negotiate with physics. Steel and copper obeyed laws that did not care about models or paperwork.

The number steadied again.

60.00.

The operators never looked worried. They had seen this dance thousands of times. To them it was routine.

To Callie, it felt like watching a tightrope walker who never looked down.

"This is the primary?" she asked quietly.

Dale nodded. "Yes, primary. The secondary's in Ohio. Tertiary in Arizona. Same view, different building."

Redundancy layered on redundancy. Power supplies fed from independent substations. There were diesel generators housed below grade and battery rooms she would never see. The building itself looked like a conference center from the outside. Inside, it was the brainstem of the electrical grid.

She watched the frequency again. A slight deviation. A correction. She thought about Sentinel Creek and the aging 7E, and her black start diesels she maintained more faithfully than many maintain their health. Out there, machines strained, leaked, and vibrated. In here they became abstractions, colored lines, margins, and assumptions.

The amber line returned. Longer this time. Still, no one spoke. The operator's jaw tightened almost imperceptibly. Another setpoint shifted. A hydro unit upstream came off its lower limit. The amber line faded.

Callie felt something she had not expected. Scale. Not the scale of megawatts. She knew megawatts. She spent a career fighting for them. This was the scale of consequence. If this room were wrong, everyone would know. If this room was right, no one would. It was a quiet paradox.

The dimly lit wall shifted as the weather model updated. Offshore winds had strengthened. The computer forecast for load ticked upward by a fraction. No one flinched.

Dale leaned toward her slightly, speaking just above the hum.

"Most days," he said, "nothing happens."

She kept her eyes on the wall.

"And on the days it does?"

He held her gaze a moment longer than necessary. She immediately understood.

Samuel Tribetti did not look like a man who controlled anything.

He wore no tie. His badge hung slightly crooked from a frayed lanyard. A chipped, faded ceramic coffee mug with multiple stain rings in it rested near his keyboard, long since gone cold. He stood when Dale introduced them, shook Callie's hand, and sat back down without ceremony.

"Dale tells me you're the plant manager at Sentinel Creek."

"Yes," Callie said. "Combined cycle. Black start designated."

Samuel nodded once. "Dependable plant. Fast ramp. You're one of the good guys."

She glanced at the massive glowing wall with the system mimic on it. "Impressive view."

"It's just data," he said. "The impressive part is when it behaves."

His eyes brightened momentarily.

The amber oscillation indicator flickered again, apparently not enough to escalate, but enough to notice.

Callie waited until it settled.

"I'm curious, how often do you re-verify black start units?" she asked.

Samuel didn't look surprised by the question. "We ask for monthly testing with the required documentation submitted through the compliance portal. Every few years we run full-scale exercises with selected plants."

"Do you ever witness them?"

"Sometimes." He swiveled slightly toward her. "We audit a sample. But we rely on certification. When you, as a plant manager sign a readiness attestation, that carries legal weight."

Dale folded his arms. "You obviously can't be everywhere."

Samuel shook his head. "Not hardly. I am certain that if we tried, the system would just grind to a halt. We must operate on declared capability."

"Declared," Callie turned her head slightly and repeated.

"It's the only way a system this size functions." He gestured toward the wall. "We coordinate thousands of megawatts across multiple states. Transmission owners, generation owners, load-serving entities. We verify through process."

Another operator leaned forward at the next console, making a slight adjustment. A gas turbine at High Mesa eased off its upper limit by a fraction. The frequency box trembled and steadied.

Samuel watched it without drama.

"What keeps you up at night?" Callie asked.

He chuffed a cynical laugh, not answering immediately.

"Assumptions," he finally said.

Dale glanced at him.

Samuel continued. “We assume the models reflect reality. We assume telemetry is accurate. We assume units designated as black start will perform as studied. We live our lives with assumptions.”

“And if they don’t?” Callie asked quietly.

“Then restoration takes longer. People and businesses are in the dark. Trust me. It’s not a good day.”

He grinned and shook his head a bit.

He pointed toward a lower screen displaying a restoration sequence diagram. Lines faded from red to gray, then back to energized blue as the simulation ran.

“In a full collapse, we bring up designated black start units. Energize transmission corridors. Establish islands. Synchronize. Expand. It’s procedural.”

“And if one of the designated units doesn’t start?” Dale asked.

Samuel shrugged slightly. “We move to the next resource in the sequence. It’s the only thing we can do.”

"Assuming the next one starts," Callie said.

He looked at her for the first time without the distraction of screens.

"They usually do. These are the assumptions the whole system rests on."

The room remained quiet.

Callie studied the wall again. Colored lines pulsed with quiet authority. Load curves bent and corrected in real time. Weather rotated offshore in muted greens.

"Do you run training drills?" she asked.

"We do tabletops quarterly and full simulations annually. We stress the system harder than nature does most years."

"And the plants?" she pressed gently.

"They certify participation." He paused. "Compliance is monitored through NERC standards."

He said it as a fact, not defense.

Dale leaned slightly toward the console. "At the plant level, readiness can mean different things."

Samuel nodded. “I know.”

He did not elaborate.

Another amber flicker appeared. Longer this time. The operator adjusted a setpoint without looking flustered.

The frequency dipped.

59.97.

Recovered.

Samuel watched the correction, satisfied.

“We are very good at managing what we can see,” he said.

Callie felt the weight of the words without accusation in them.

“And what you can’t?” she asked.

He returned his attention to the wall.

“That’s why we require certification.”

No one in the room reacted to the conversation. The grid continued to move in disciplined geometry.

Dale glanced at Callie. She understood the exchange had reached its natural end.

Samuel extended his hand again as they prepared to leave the operations floor.

He looked at Callie and smiled broadly.

“If you ever want to participate in a restoration exercise from the plant side, let us know. We’re always looking for helpful, engaged operators.”

“I might take you up on that,” she said.

As they stepped back through the security doors, the hum of ventilation softened behind them.

Outside, the building looked unremarkable. Glass and steel. Neutral landscaping. No hint of the authority inside.

Callie turned to Dale.

“They’re doing everything right,” she said.

“Yes,” he replied.

She looked back at the building one last time.

“They’re assuming we are too.” Nothing more needed to be said.

On the way back to Millstone Junction Dale glanced at Callie with a smile on his face.

"Trying not to sound like a snob, but the diner in Millstone Junction is a little rough."

Callie immediately laughed.

"It is a local thing. I don't think it has ever been any good, but it stays busy. It is like the center of that little town. The locals think it's great."

With a touch of trepidation, he looked at her again.

"I know a very nice steak and seafood house in the city. I don't get to go often, but it has never disappointed."

Callie panicked for a moment.

"Dale, I am not dressed for something real fancy."

"Did I say it was fancy? I don't think it falls into the fancy category as much as just a good place to eat." He paused and glanced at her again. "Besides, an attractive woman is attractive no matter what she's wearing." He winced in his mind immediately thinking, what just rolled out of my mouth?

Callie slowly reached over and squeezed his arm gently with a smile.

"For someone who is very technical and business minded, you can be very charming."

He visibly exhaled and relaxed.

She kept her eyes ahead as she quietly said, "Dale, I would be delighted to have dinner with you."

He didn't return her to Millstone Junction until very late that evening. The streets of Millstone Junction were quiet when he pulled to the curb in front of her mother's house. The porch light had been left on. He hoped it was courtesy and not surveillance.

Dale shifted the truck into park but did not immediately reach for the door handle.

"I'm glad you came today," he said softly.

"So am I," she replied.

Neither moved.

The engine ticked softly as it cooled. Somewhere down the block a dog barked once and then stopped. The night felt still in a way that made leaving difficult.

Callie reached for the door handle, then paused. She turned back toward him. The look wasn't dramatic. It was peaceful and steady.

"Thank you," she said. "For today."

He nodded once. "We're on the same side."

"I know."

That moment lingered between them.

He stepped out first and walked her to the porch. It wasn't chivalry as much as reluctance to let the evening end.

At the bottom step she turned toward him. He stood close enough now that he could smell the faint trace of her perfume beneath the cool night air.

He gave her space to step back.

She didn't.

The kiss was brief. Not searching. Not hesitant, but certain.

When they separated, she rested her forehead lightly against his chest for just a moment, her hand still on his sleeve.

Nothing was spoken. There was nothing to negotiate.

She stepped back first.

“Good night, Dale.”

“Good night, Callie.”

He watched her reach the door and disappear inside before walking back to the truck.

As he drove away, he realized he felt aligned for the first time in years.

***

Part 8

E-Mail

****

Returning to Sentinel Creek after the System Operations Center visit was more difficult than Callie expected. She told herself Dale Morrison was a distraction. That explanation was convenient, but it wasn't entirely true. She could not get him off her mind. She forced herself back into her work.

Sentinel Creek had responsibilities that went far beyond its modest megawatt rating. If something ever went wrong on the grid, this plant might matter a great deal. She decided to run several readiness checks.

Performing live load tests on her diesels and the LM-2500 always felt rewarding. She felt a rush of pride, a quiet confirmation that the effort to keep the plant ready mattered. The tests today flushed several very small issues out of both systems. She analyzed the issues and corrected them immediately. She was obsessive about readiness. If the grid ever needed Sentinel Creek, it would start.

Now what?

After pondering the state of the Twin-Pac for hours, she decided to call Teddy Warnick. No answer. She left a few messages, but he didn't reply. This was disappointing to her. After what she witnessed on her visit to Franklin Generating Station, her present knowledge of the situation would not allow her to relax.

She defaulted to re-studying grid interconnections and substations for several hours. It only made her more uncomfortable with the state of readiness if something were to happen. She decided to see if she could find something on the MidAtlantic corporate intranet.

She went to the corporate compliance server. After a lengthy search, she was shocked to see that the black start Twin-Pac at Franklin Generating Station showed five years of successful monthly tests, including the bi-annual loading tests. She knew that could not be correct.

Samuel Tribetti's words haunted her over and over:

"When you, as a plant manager, sign a readiness attestation, that carries legal weight."

She called Dale. He answered immediately.

"Hey Callie, how are you doing?" His voice upbeat. He was pleased to hear from her.

"Good. Do you have a few minutes? I need to tell you something."

"Of course. What's going on?" She could feel his sincerity.

"Can I send you some documents that I found on the corporate compliance server?"

"Absolutely. Is there an issue?" His concern was real.

"Dale, Teddy Warnick has signed three years of successful test data, including load tests, that can't possibly be real. One of the ICE techs and his Ops Manager even told me they had problems with the unit."

“That’s not good.” He paused and lowered his voice. “Not good at all.”

He redirected for a moment.

“From everything I hear, Teddy is in trouble at Franklin. There have been too many calls to Human Resources. HR has raised several flags.”

He thought for a moment before continuing.

“I hate speculation but the VP of fossil generation, your boss, Anthony Newson and Teddy are good friends. You have worked for Anthony long enough to know what that means.”

Callie grimaced. She knew Anthony well. He had passed over her for the Plant Manager’s position multiple times because she was too “inexperienced.” Oddly, the previous plant manager at Sentinel Creek was two years younger than her and had five years less experience. Yes, she knew Anthony.

They both knew it was time to return the subject back to Franklin’s black start issue. Callie responded first.

"As you know, I am being ghosted by Kendall Allen's group. I am not sure what to do." She paused to choose the right words. "Do I leave it alone, or do I take some kind of action?"

"Callie… what does your gut tell you?"

"Frankly, it's driving me nuts. SOC was impressive, Dale, but we both know they're dealing with faulty data." She paused. "Samuel Tribetti made it clear they depend on the assumptions of readiness and testing."

Dale had to think for a few moments.

"First of all, I really appreciate you calling me. I feel like we are in this together. Have you considered a well-placed e-mail to Teddy?"

"He won't return my calls, but maybe an e-mail would be appropriate."

"I know you will be careful in the e-mail to not make accusations, but I think you need to make it clear that there is a problem."

They talked for several more minutes before ending the call. Callie went straight to her computer and sent the signed attestations to Dale and then crafted an e-mail to Teddy. She rewrote it several times until it carried the right tone and weight.

***

Subject: Franklin Twin-Pac Black Start Documentation

Teddy,

I'm sorry we were unable to connect during my recent visit to Franklin Energy Center. Alex, Eric, and Mike were generous with their time and helpful in walking me through current procedures.

As you know, I've been reviewing fleet-wide black start readiness as part of the corporate restoration procedure update. During my visit, I noted several operational concerns regarding the Twin-Pac unit that may affect declared start timelines under certain conditions.

While reviewing the MARES attestations on the compliance server, I observed that the monthly and bi-annual load tests have been reported as fully successful over the past several years. Based on conversations during my visit, I would appreciate clarification to ensure the documentation and field experience are aligned.

If you have time this week, I would welcome a brief call to discuss.

Regards,

Callie McGraw

Plant Manager

Sentinel Creek Generating Station

***

She sent the e-mail to Dale to review. He called almost immediately.

"Got the e-mail for Teddy. I think it looks good. Very professional and non-inflammatory. Have you sent it to him yet?"

"No, I wanted your input first. I don't know Teddy, you do. Just making certain I wasn't raising a red flag."

"I see no reason to not send it. Also, I don't really know him that well. I have talked with him at a few meetings and gave him a tour at Torlon Hills a couple of years ago." He smiled. "He didn't get the VIP tour you did, though."

Callie laughed.

"There's no question, I got the deluxe tour and I do appreciate it!"

After ending the call with Dale, she read the e-mail aloud once more and then hit SEND apprehensively. She went home that evening and tried to put it out of mind.

Teddy didn't see the e-mail until the next morning. He read it. He read it again. He immediately called Eric Royden, the Maintenance Manager, and Mike Cummings the Operations Manager into his office. They had barely sat down before he laid into them.

"Exactly what in the hell did either of you tell Callie McGraw when she visited the plant a few days ago?" His anger was loudly evident.

Eric spoke first.

"I didn't say much. I was busy and had Alex Cordon take her to see the Twin-Pac. I didn't see her after that." He paused and then raised his head. "She did tell me that she was on PTO and just visiting. I remember this clearly because I gave her a hard time about it."

Mike listened to Eric's explanation and shook his head defensively.

"She asked a ton of questions, digging me about the Twin-Pac. I told her that sometimes we have problems during the tests."

Teddy raised his voice.

"Did you explicitly tell her that we have not had a successful load test during the previous few testing cycles?"

Mike was struggling. He had never cared for Teddy or his management style. Teddy's reputation was well known. He would turn on you in a heartbeat if it benefited him politically. He had been through more Ops Managers than anyone in the MidAtlantic system. No one could understand how he kept the Plant Manager position at Franklin Energy Center. It was considered the flagship of the fleet but its issues were quietly multiplying.

He shook his head, looked aggressively into Teddy's eyes and answered defensively.

"I don't remember. It was just small talk. I don't think I told her any specifics, just that we have had a few minor problems in the past with starts and loading."

Teddy glared at him.

"Why would you tell her anything? She has nothing to do with this plant. I think in the future you need to be damn careful about what you tell anyone outside of this plant. Do you understand what I am saying?"

Mike's anger quietly flared. Teddy could be the most condescending person he ever knew. When he accepted the Ops Manager job, it was simply to pad his résumé in an effort to get out of Franklin. He now questioned daily if it was worth it. Especially if he went the way of the previous two Ops Managers that Teddy openly crucified.

Teddy then looked angrily at Eric.

"Is Alex Cordon here today?"

Eric stiffened.

"Yes, I saw him about an hour ago in the instrument shop."

"Ask him to come to my office NOW!"

He turned back toward Mike.

"No one, under any circumstance should EVER discuss anything with that fucking Callie McGraw unless I explicitly okay it." He paused. "I hope I make myself damn clear!"

Eric and Mike left Teddy's office seething. Teddy made working at Franklin extremely difficult. Mike on more than one occasion had considered simply walking out of the plant and not returning.

Several minutes later Alex leaned into his office and pensively said, "Did you want to see me?"

Teddy's temper was still smoldering.

"Sit down, Alex." He took a drink of his now lukewarm coffee.

"You took Callie McGraw out to the Twin-Pac during her site visit a few days back. I want to know exactly what was said and what she looked at. Don't leave anything out."

In restrained, fearful cadence Alex outlined the visit to the Twin-Pac, including opening the doors and finding the exhaust drain closed and all the oil booms from the leaking generator seals. When he finished, Teddy addressed him one more time.

"Did you tell her anything about the operational tests failing?"

Alex thought for a few moments.

"I told her about that Agastat timer relay that we had difficulties finding, but that was all."

Teddy stared angrily at Alex for a few moments.

"You need to get back to work now." He raised his voice. "One other thing, don't you ever give information about this plant to anyone outside of this plant. Do you understand?"

"Yes sir, I do sir."

Alex quickly left his office.

Teddy wasted no time. He emailed Garrin Storz, Kendall Allen's second-in- command. He copied Shane Holowell and Justin Edwards, both electrical engineers who were working with the corporate black start procedures before Kendall took over from Joel Adamson.

***

Subject: Callie McGraw – Franklin Twin-Pac

Garrin,

Callie McGraw visited Franklin last week and accessed our Twin-Pac black start unit without prior coordination or approval from me. After her visit, she accessed compliance documentation related to MARES attestations and has now questioned the declared test results based on her limited site exposure.

Before responding, I would appreciate clarity regarding her official role in the corporate black start procedure. Under Joel Adamson, she appeared to be involved in some capacity. Does she currently have an authorized function in this area?

Additionally, I understand she recently visited the MARES SOC and was accompanied by Dale Morrison from Torlon Hills. I would appreciate clarification regarding the scope and coordination of these activities. For the record, I believe her visit here and to the SOC was classified as PTO and not company paid. This concerns me.

Given the regulatory sensitivity surrounding black start attestations, I want to ensure all communication channels and authority lines are clear before engaging further.

Sincerely,

Teddy Warnick

Plant Manager

Franklin Energy Center

Teddy read the message once more before hitting send. Teddy leaned back in his chair and stared at the wall. The problem was not the Twin-Pac. The problem was Callie McGraw.

***

Part 9

Fallout Begins

****

Garrin Storz received and read Teddy Warnick's e-mail the next morning. He knew that Callie had done some piecemeal work on the black start procedure when Joel Adamson was still the VP of transmission. He called the two engineers most involved with the procedure into his office: Shane Hollowell and Justin Edwards.

"Gentlemen, I assume you saw Teddy Warnick's e-mail about Callie McGraw."

Both acknowledged.

"What do either of you know about this situation?"

Shane answered first.

"She was deeply involved when Joel was VP. She's sharp, surprisingly insightful, but she never had a formal role. The procedure is administered from this office."

Justin nodded in agreement.

"I was the original lead on this. I used Callie as a resource because her plant, Sentinel Creek, is the other black start unit." He thought for a moment.

"I believe Joel just designated her as a resource, nothing more. I do know that she was vocal about it not being sufficient and that it didn't address enough contingencies."

He shook his head and then continued.

"For God's sake Garrin, you know the mathematical permutations possible with this. You've seen the modeling. She wanted several different procedures based on different contingencies. I decided this was above and beyond our obligation to MARES. I related this to her in an e-mail earlier this year, but she apparently doesn't want to let it go. I guess that's where she picked up the nickname, Bulldog."

Shane smiled momentarily and interjected.

"What the hell is she doing visiting MARES and Franklin Energy Center on personal time and asking these questions?"

Garrin shrugged his shoulders.

"That's all I needed. I will take it from here. I need to speak to Kendall about this. I would simply dismiss this, but I don't have a clue why she would be digging through the compliance reports. That concerns me."

Later, Garrin met with Kendall. Kendall was alarmed. Alarmed enough to check payroll records after Garrin's visit. Both Dale and Callie had visited the MARES SOC on personal time, and Callie's visit to Franklin was also recorded as PTO.

Kendall called Cal Johnson, VP of nuclear.

"Cal, Kendall Allen here. How are you doing today?"

"Good, Kendall. What's on your mind?"

"I am dealing with a sensitive matter that could leave us exposed. Dale Morrison visited the MARES SOC on his personal time with Callie McGraw last week. She is the plant manager of the Sentinel Creek plant. Immediately afterwards, Callie apparently went onto the compliance server and downloaded all the black start test records from Franklin without Teddy Warnick's permission or knowledge. I know Torlon Hills is in a major outage right now. Why would Dale be taking time off with Callie McGraw to visit MARES during this time?"

Cal was caught off guard. As an attorney, he didn't like being caught off guard.

"Kendall, I have no idea what this is about. I will discuss this with Dale. It might be wise to call Anthony Newson, the fossil VP and let him know what is going on. He may want to discuss this with Callie McGraw."

Cal wasted no time. He looked to Langford as an ally. Langford was in the control room during the scram debacle when Dale was giving the tour. Plus, the extended refueling outage at Torlon Hills was going south due to issues. Cal decided he would take action. He called Dale into corporate headquarters.

There was a chill in Cal's office as Dale sat in the plush, leather chair in front of Cal's oversized mahogany desk.

"Dale, we've had our differences, but you are a good plant manager. We are concerned about several issues, but the biggest problem is the outage at Torlon Hills is not going well. We are taking a big hit to the bottom line."

Dale held steady as always.

"Cal, we are paying now for deferred maintenance with the budget cuts. I warned you on several occasions we may be setting ourselves up for failure."

Dale straightened slightly and looked directly into Cal's eyes.

"Pay me now or pay me later. Our assessed-risk assumptions clearly reveal what it costs to keep these plants operating."

Cal's anger flared.

"Our assessed-risk assumptions implied proper management of these risks. Did we manage them properly?"

Dale never flinched.

"We did. We still lost. The turbine rotor cracks should have been addressed when you deferred the maintenance. Steel doesn't heal over time, Cal."

"Be that as it may, we have another issue that may be even more problematic."

Dale sat attentively, not knowing what was next.

"Did you visit the MARES SOC with Callie McGraw on your personal time last week?"

"I did. Callie had never seen it and she, in my opinion, has been instrumental in the development of the corporate black start procedure."

"You don't see this as a conflict?" Cal's voice now reflected his irritation.

"She downloaded compliance records from Franklin Energy Center without permission or consultation with Teddy Warnick. What am I supposed to think here?"

He paused to let the question settle.

"You are overseeing an outage that is costing the company a substantial amount of money and right in the middle of it you take time off to do something with a procedure that is administered here, in this building, with a person that technically should not be involved at all."

Dale understood what this meeting was really about from the moment Cal mentioned the SOC visit. He was not backing down.

"Sentinel Creek is one of two black start units in the entire MidAtlantic system. Callie McGraw is the plant manager of Sentinel Creek and trying to do the right thing. She is ensuring that we are ready in the event of a system collapse."

Cal shook his head.

"Dale, do you have something going with this woman? Is your judgement clouded?"

"Not at all. I think she is onto something that leaves us wide open for issues."

Cal made his final decision. He wasn't sure when the meeting started which way things would go, but he was certain now.

"Dale, we have discussed this internally and are reassigning you to Silver Ridge Energy Center as plant manager. You will, of course, be working under Anthony Newson, the VP of fossil generation. We are moving Marvin Chandler from the plant manager position at Redstone Valley Nuclear to Torlon Hills. This is effective immediately."

Dale felt gut-punched. However, he maintained his composure.

"Just like that, I am out of nuclear?"

"Dale, you are an excellent man. You just need to get your priorities in order. Silver Ridge can use your expertise." He paused. "After today you will report directly to Anthony Newson, the VP of fossil generation.

Dale left Cal's office with a pit deep in his stomach. His first call was to Callie. He waited until he was alone in his truck.

"Callie, I was just moved to Silver Ridge as the plant manager."

A pause.

"When?"

"Immediately."

Another pause.

"I'm so sorry," she said.

"Yeah, me too."

They ended the call without trying to solve anything. Dale had been in nuclear his entire career. Silver Ridge was fossil. A reassignment without the word demotion.

She stared at the black-start binder on her desk. Her vision blurred as a few hot tears slid slowly down her cheeks. A sharp breath caught in her chest. She wiped her eyes once, almost irritated with herself, and forced the feeling back where it belonged.

Steel and iron do not care about politics, mathematical models do not care about pride, and storms do not care about hierarchy. She stood, squared the papers on her desk, and went back to work.

The next day, Anthony Newson, the VP of fossil generation arrived at Sentinel Creek unannounced. His previous visit was years earlier when he was head of the legal department. Callie was a staff engineer then. He didn't even know her name.

Anthony Newson was an anomaly in MidAtlantic Energy. He had started in the plants as an entry-level operator and climbed steadily upward while better-credentialed people came and went.

He understood machinery well enough, but he understood organizations even better.

When the mergers reshaped MidAtlantic, Anthony had simply been the last man still standing in the right chair.

Sentinel Creek was the smallest of his plants, and the furthest away from corporate. Because of its size and location, and because it was usually the least troublesome of the plants, it was normally off his radar.

Since being awarded the plant manager position, Callie worked hard improving the image of Sentinel Creek Generating Station. Even with the budget issues, she managed to paint the plant, cleaning it up to look new. One of her talented operators had, with her permission, painted a mural of the picturesque Sentinel Creek meandering through the trees on the side of the maintenance shop. The plant had never looked better.

Callie was in her office when Anthony knocked at the door.

"Callie, do you have a few minutes?"

She wasn't surprised after Dale's call yesterday.

"Of course. Please sit down. Can I get you some coffee?"

"No. I'm fine."

"How can I help you today?"

"Callie, there is concern at the corporate level about your persistence in pursuing changes to the corporate black start procedure." He paused. "Particularly about your visit to Franklin Energy Center and the MARES SOC on your days off."

Her voice remained steady, unemotional.

"Anthony, my folks live in Millstone Junction. My visit was to them. Because I was there, I thought it would be interesting to see Franklin since they are the other black start facility. The SOC visit was a bonus. I had never seen it before."

He squinted and lowered his voice.

"Callie, we don't have a problem with that as much as we do with your tampering with legal documents on the corporate compliance server."

Callie did not react immediately. She let the word tampering settle in the air between them.

"Anthony," she said evenly, "I accessed records available to plant managers across the fleet. I did not alter them. I reviewed them."

He studied her.

"That documentation involves regulatory attestations to MARES. Those are not casual files."

"I understand that," she replied. "Which is precisely why I reviewed them."

Anthony leaned back slightly in his chair.

"You weren't assigned to audit Franklin Energy Center."

"No," she agreed. "But Sentinel Creek is a designated black start facility. If restoration depends on declared capabilities across the fleet, then discrepancies affect all of us."

He narrowed his eyes.

"Discrepancies."

She nodded once.

"The attestations reflect five years of fully successful monthly and bi-annual load tests. Field conversations indicated repeated starting and loading issues. I simply asked for clarification."

"But that's not your role."

"Black start readiness is my role," she asserted. "Restoration modeling assumes declared timelines. If the inputs are inaccurate, the restoration sequence is inaccurate."

Anthony's jaw tightened slightly.

"You are creating exposure."

Callie held his gaze.

"Exposure already exists if declared capability does not match operational reality."

Silence filled the office for several seconds.

Anthony shifted tone.

"This procedure is administered at the corporate level. If there are concerns, they should be routed through this office."

"I understand," she said. "Going forward I will coordinate formally. My intent was not to bypass authority."

"Your intent is not the issue," he replied. "Perception is."

She did not answer.

He continued.

"You will refrain from independent access of compliance records outside your plant unless explicitly directed. You will also suspend any direct communication with other plant managers regarding black start documentation without corporate involvement."

A measured pause.

"Is that clear?"

"Yes."

"And Callie…" he added, softer now, but no less firm, "initiative is valued. But discipline is required."

She rose from her chair.

"I have no interest in creating instability, Anthony. Only in preventing it."

He gave a thin nod.

"We all do." He smiled and stood from his chair. "The plant is looking good, Callie. I like the mural, it is a nice touch."

He shook her hand and left the site.

As soon as Anthony left the gate, Callie called Dale. He was home. He answered on the first ring.

"Dale, this is Callie. How are you doing today?"

He chuffed a disingenuous laugh.

"Licking my wounds."

"I get it." She paused. "I just had an in-person visit from Anthony Newson."

Dale perked up.

"Is this unusual?"

"Very. In my entire time at Sentinel Creek, this is only the second time he has been here."

"What is going on?"

"You were assigned to Silver Ridge. I was just put into check. I was told I was to no longer discuss black start, or black start related items with anyone."

Dale's anger surged.

"That is ridiculous. It makes no sense whatsoever."

"Apparently the e-mail I sent to Teddy stirred things that should have been left unsaid?"

"No, Callie, they needed saying. You didn't do anything wrong."

There was an extended pause.

"Dale, where do we go from here?"

"I am not sure. I have learned that when I am feeling like I am right now to not make any big decisions. I think this is good wisdom for both of us to follow."

"I agree. I wish you were here."

"Me too."

Outside, the plant hummed as it always had. Steel, steam, and rotating mass. None of it aware of perception, scope, or authority.

***

Part 10

The Storm

****

The first warning arrived quietly enough that no one noticed it for what it was. Two days after Dale Morrison's reassignment became official, the atmospheric charts over the eastern United States began developing a shape meteorologists disliked.

Orville Donovan's earlier concerns were now reality. The jet stream dipped farther south than seasonal models had predicted, forming a slow, deep trough stretching from the Great Lakes down toward the Appalachian spine.

To most forecasters it looked like nothing more than a typical late-winter pattern adjustment. To the small group of grid reliability engineers who paid attention to weather maps, it meant something else entirely.

Ice.

Heavy ice.

Not the decorative kind that glazed tree branches and melted by afternoon. This kind of storm built slowly in layers, accumulating weight hour after hour until steel structures began to notice.

Two hundred miles away at the MARES System Operations Center, the night transmission desk noticed something different. The Hudson 345 kV corridor had begun loading higher than normal during overnight hours. Not dramatically. Nothing that would trigger alarms. Just a slow climb in MVAR flow that did not match the typical seasonal profile. The Hudson path was quietly picking up transfers the 500 kV corridor normally carried.

The operator tagged the line in his log: Unusual loading trend.

He assumed it would correct itself during the morning dispatch cycle.

At Sentinel Creek, Callie McGraw was dealing with something much smaller. During the morning equipment walkdown, one of the auxiliary diesel generators failed to start on its first attempt during a routine surveillance test. It started immediately on the second try. The control room logged the event and moved on. A single delayed start was not unusual for a machine that spent most of its life waiting for emergencies.

Callie reviewed the test report later that afternoon. She circled the start time in red pen. Something about the delay bothered her. Not enough to raise an alarm. Just enough to write a small note in the margin of the page. Verify air start pressure trend.

Outside, the sky over the Appalachian corridor continued to darken as the developing weather system gathered strength. Across three states, steel transmission towers stood quietly in frozen fields. They had no opinion about atmospheric pressure. They only cared about weight.

After the reassignment pushed Dale out of Torlon Hills, he immediately put his house on the market and rented a small apartment near Silver Ridge Energy Center. He was still struggling with the demotion and wondering whether he would remain with MidAtlantic at all. Fortunately, the reassignment did not come with a pay cut. In fact, he now sat several steps above the highest compensation tier for a fossil plant manager. It simply meant his salary had nowhere left to go.

Silver Ridge had been built after Franklin but with fewer embellishments. Franklin received an expansive maintenance shop, landscaped entrances, and oversized conference facilities. Silver Ridge was functional, efficient, and unadorned.

Like Franklin, it consisted of two 2x1 combined-cycle blocks capable of producing roughly 1,200 megawatts depending on ambient conditions. Technically they were nearly identical. Silver Ridge, built second, benefited from lessons learned during Franklin's startup. Overall, it was a well-designed facility, though cost cutting had taken a toll.

Though their plants were several hours apart, Dale and Callie spoke daily. The calls were measured and practical at first, then gradually less so. They did not discuss what had been taken from him. They discussed systems, weather, staffing, and the small absurdities of corporate life. Those conversations became the most stable part of each day, the part both of them looked forward to most. Their bond was growing daily.

Downsizing from a house to a small apartment required decisions. Much of his furniture, tools, and garage equipment would go into storage. The remaining would be transported to the apartment.

On his daily call to Callie, he complained about how much of his life was headed for storage. Callie took this moment to let him know her plans.

"I am coming to help you finish your move. You sound like you could use the company."

He wanted to see her, but it didn't seem practical at this time.

"Callie, that's not necessary. The trip is long and the weather is unsettled."

"Nonsense. I have made up my mind. You need the help and I want to help. This equation balances perfectly. Be sure to leave something for me to do."

Dale half-heartedly tried to talk her out of it but was pleased she didn't listen.

On the afternoon the last of his belongings were transported by the movers to storage, Callie arrived. She stepped out of her car as he carried a box toward the moving truck.

"You didn't think I'd let you do this alone, did you?"

He set the box down. They embraced without hesitation. The hug lingered far longer than either intended. It was not dramatic, but familiar in a way neither of them had permitted before. When they separated, neither commented. They both understood the sincerity of their connection.

With most of his belongings in storage, they loaded the remaining boxes and made the two-hour trip to his new apartment. It was a steel gray, cold and windy day late in February. They were recovering from a recent cold snap that dramatically increased the natural gas and fuel oil prices in the region.

They unloaded the truck of his personal belongings as quickly as possible. The cold and the wind cut right through them. Dale quietly relished her help, and Callie was glad to be there.

She wanted to see the Silver Ridge plant, but they decided that the recent issues warranted discretion. Besides, Block 1 was offline with a major thrust bearing repair on the steam turbine. She would just visit it some other time during a return trip in the future. They would wait until after Anthony Newson dialed down the heat he currently had on them.

The television news channels were warning of a possibly significant storm headed their way. They watched carefully for changes and simply enjoyed their time together.

She was close enough to Millstone Junction that her original plan was to spend an evening at her parent's house. Unintentionally, her time with Dale pushed the home visit off the docket. Plus, the promised weather disturbance was moving quicker than most thought it would.

That evening Dale finally broke down his feelings about MidAtlantic to Callie.

"They want me out," he said bluntly. "They know I have been nuclear my entire career. I think Cal would have fired me, but Anthony needed to fill the plant manager position at Silver Ridge. I was a convenient casualty."

"Do you know what you want to do?"

Dale didn't answer immediately. He thought about it and then chose his words carefully.

"Callie, I want to start my own consulting firm. I've been thinking about it for quite some time. It would let me get out from under MidAtlantic politics and do what I love best."

He turned and looked directly into her eyes with a smile.

“Frankly, I would like to move five or six hours west of here, somewhere near Sentinel Creek, and open a consulting company.”

Callie realized this was more of an announcement than a statement.

“Dale, I think that would be wonderful.”

They locked eyes and smiled at each other. Callie broke the silence.

“Sit down in that chair.” She pointed to a wooden chair that matched the small kitchen table they carried into the apartment earlier. She began massaging his shoulders. They were tight and knotted. He groaned as she used her elbow, trying to release the knotted muscles in his upper back.

“Callie, that is amazing.”

After several minutes she slowly, quietly said, "your muscles are far too tense. I think it will take some heat to release them."

"Heat?"

She leaned over, putting her lips right to his ear and whispered quietly, slowly:

"A hot shower massage."

The following morning, they unboxed his toaster and feasted on peanut butter toast and black coffee. Their connection was intense. For the first time in many years both Callie and Dale felt whole. They remained at the apartment that day, relaxing and watching the weather.

As conditions deteriorated, they decided it was best for her not to attempt the drive back to Sentinel Creek. The forecasters were predicting ice. Possibly significant ice. There are few seemingly perfect days in life. This day felt like one to both of them.

On the wall monitors at the MARES System Operations Center, the weather overlays were usually just greens and yellows drifting across the screen, the kind of visual noise operators learned to ignore unless it moved with intent.

This one had intent.

The first thing that made people look twice wasn't the color. It was the shape. A broad, cold dome was settling south from Canada, dense and stubborn, the kind of air that didn't slide politely out of the way when warmer air tried to move in. It pressed down into the valleys and pooled against the Appalachians. The meteorologists called it "cold air damming." The operators didn't call it anything. They just knew it meant the same thing it always meant. Ice, not snow, and always in the wrong places.

In the morning SOC briefing, the grid itself was calm. Generation was normal. Load was seasonably high and steady, a winter plateau. The forecast load curve didn't spike sharply the way it did on a July afternoon, but it sat heavy and continuous. People required steady home heating. Plants of various types were running as usual. Everything stayed warm by burning something.

In the MARES day-ahead report, a note appeared in the reliability section, short and overly careful:

Potential for widespread freezing rain in northern zone. Wind gusts increasing coastal. Evaluate transmission exposure.

No exclamation points. No bold warning banners. Just another line in a long document showing that someone had noticed.

Samuel Tribetti had seen weather do damage before. Not the cinematic kind. The slow, humiliating kind. Ice that didn't look particularly dramatic but brought down structures built to withstand hurricanes. Wind that found the one corroded bolt. Trees that fell onto lines that had no right to be below trees in the first place. Ice was his nemesis. While sitting at his desk, he watched the pressure forecast numbers shift by one millibar, then two. Nothing about it felt sudden. That was the uncomfortable part. The storm was not sneaking in. It was assembling.

Over the ocean, a low was forming in the way they often did, born from a harmless-looking wave along a boundary, fed by warm water and upper-level support. The models showed it coming inland first, dragging rain, then redeveloping offshore as the cold air pressed down. The old-timers called that a "Miller-B," like naming a problem made it manageable.

The meteorologists didn't argue the label. They argued the track. Thirty miles one direction and it would be a snowstorm. Thirty miles the other and it would be a freezing rain event with wind. There was always an argument about where that line was. The line mattered. It could make an incredible difference in how they administered the grid.

At MARES, the line was not a weather map thing. It was a power thing. It ran across specific corridors and specific interfaces. It ran across structures built way back in the seventies, but with modern expectations and modern loading. It ran across places where the right-of-way had narrowed over decades as trees grew back and property owners pushed. It ran across that long northern transfer spine built around the Setab 500 kV corridor and its supporting Hudson 345 kV network, a system everyone treated like it could take whatever the grid asked of it, mainly because it usually did.

By the afternoon, the first conference call happened. It sat somewhere between routine and threat. It wasn't called an emergency. It was called a "weather coordination call," and it included transmission owners, generating stations, and the handful of people in each group who always ended up on these calls no matter the holiday or the hour.

A meteorologist from a vendor service spoke in measured terms.

"Confidence is increasing in rapid intensification," she said. "We're seeing strong upper-level divergence and a tightening gradient. Some models deepen the coastal low more than 24 millibars in 24 hours."

There was a pause, as if she expected the phrase to land on people. The phrase had a definition. Bombogenesis. A "bomb cyclone" if you wanted the headline term. It meant the atmosphere was doing something fast enough to get its own name. The pressure was dropping hard and fast. The winds were rising, and everything was tightening. Samuel watched the operators as they listened. No one looked alarmed. They looked attentive.

"What's the ice accretion forecast?" someone asked from the transmission group.

"Potential for one to two inches in the northern tier," the meteorologist said. "But the range is wide. The line between snow and freezing rain remains sensitive to track and warm nose depth."

Warm nose. A layer of warm air aloft that melted snow into rain, only to have it refreeze on contact with the cold surface. It sounded almost harmless. It was how you got heavy, clear ice that coated everything and did not fall off politely.

"Wind timing?" another voice asked.

"Peak winds likely coincide with heaviest precipitation in the coastal plain. Inland gusts could still reach forty to fifty. Coastal seventy plus is possible."

No one said, "that will bring lines down." They didn't have to. Everyone on the call had seen what fifty-mile-per-hour gusts did to ice-laden conductors. The wind didn't need to be hurricane strength. Ice was always a threat with no human solution.

After the call, Samuel Tribetti paced the operations floor. He didn't rush. He didn't need to. The room was already shifting into that subtle posture it took when a day might not remain a day.

Operators pulled up contingency analysis. They ran familiar cases: N-1, then N-2, then the ones that were technically "extreme" but still lived on the hard drive because people who had been humbled kept them there.

When the study showed overloads on the northern 345 corridors after a single 500 kV outage, no one laughed. No one announced it loudly. They just stared a moment longer at the numbers. The grid didn't mind being loaded. However, it truly minded surprise.

At Sentinel Creek, weather awareness was not instinctive the way it was with rotating equipment. But Callie had taught them, painfully, that storms were not primarily meteorological events. They were logistics events. The first sign of a dangerous storm wasn't on radar. It was on a parts shelf. She pushed her people to understand the foundation of a severe weather event and how to try and stay ahead of it. She felt a twinge of guilt for not being at the plant right now.

She texted the shift on duty.

"Check the warehouse for extra fuel filters, heater elements, heat trace, and work lights. Make certain you have plenty of kerosene for the portable torpedo heaters."

She had carried the moniker of "Bulldog" for many years, having never reacted to the nickname. She just kept showing up with the same questions. Tonight was no different. She wanted the operators to be on their toes.

On the control room screens, the operators watched the load forecast tick upward slightly as the temperature projections dropped. The wind forecast ticked upward as the pressure projections dropped. The two together made a quiet kind of certainty. People would be cold. People would need power. Power would be harder to move.

The irony of her being at Dale's was not lost on her: The system needed to be at its strongest precisely when the physical world was most eager to tear it apart. She was not there for an event that could be major. Her texts with her operators proved they were watching the weather also, in the way plant operators watched anything that might change their day.

She couldn't help herself. After many preparation questions sent by text, she made a decision. She called the

Sentinel Creek control room and asked for a conference call.

"I want you to do a test run of the diesels now," she said.

"We ran 'em last week." They answered in almost unison.

"I want you to run them again."

They didn't argue. The nickname "Bulldog" had all the right connotations. They understood the difference between passing a test and being ready.

The control room operator left the control room for the diesels. The air had that dry, sharp edge that came before real cold, the kind that made metal sound different. The wind was calm, but it felt like a calm that was waiting for something to arrive.

Inside the Sentinel Creek annex, the diesels sat as they always had, large, blunt, and indifferent. Machines that truly did not care about human scheduling. The operator watched the preheat indicators, listened to the starting air, and was attentive to the first combustion. He listened to the way the engine took load. Callie had taught them properly. While they relied on the DCS data, there were things you could only feel by standing there. She had impressed on them how critical it was to be there and listen when they started.

When the diesel took the first load step cleanly, the control operator breathed a sigh of relief. He signed the test sheet with a steady hand.

That night, the storm was moving from possibility to inevitability. Local news anchors began using the word "historic." Weather services began shading maps in purple they reserved for things they were tired of underestimating. Schools began hinting at closures. Grocery stores behaved the way they always did before storms. Bread and milk disappeared first.

At MARES, the language remained flat.

"Elevated risk."

"Potential for significant outages."

"Prepare for sustained response."

Samuel didn't trust the public maps. He trusted the pressure trace. He watched the modeled central pressure fall into numbers that made the Atlantic look like an engine. He watched the gradient tighten, which meant wind.

He watched the thermal profile in the northern zone hold stubbornly below freezing at the surface while warming above. That meant ice. He shuddered. Hard.

He listened as the transmission desk talked through pre-contingency actions.

"Can we reconfigure the north corridor to reduce loading?"

"We can shift some flow, but it stresses the central 345 network."

"What about importing less from the Great Plains intertie?"

"Then we need more internal generation."

"What's available?"

Another operator answered before anyone else could. "And if Hudson starts to choke, we may have to back down Great Plains imports and lean harder on Atlantic support."

A list followed, short and more constrained than it should have been. Units were down for maintenance that had been run too long. Units that could run but were fuel-limited. Units that could ramp but were constrained by emissions permits. Units that were technically available but had chronic issues and always needed a gentle hand. It was a fleet that had been optimized. Optimized fleets abhor unusual weather.

Somewhere in the room an operator said quietly, "We should stage under-frequency load shedding early."

Samuel didn't respond. The operator wasn't wrong.

Under-frequency load shedding was not a plan. It was an admission that the system might not hold. It was also a tool that saved grids on a consistent basis. The problem was that it saved them by hurting people. When the frequency drops, you just dump part of the load. This works well unless you are in the area that was dumped.

At Torlon Hills, the outage continued the way most outages do, by resisting management's desire to control it. It was a refueling outage. But "routine" inspections revealed the cost of deferred maintenance. In this case, there were unanticipated cracks in the LP turbine rotor. The schedule shifted. The calls became tighter. The tone of the outage meetings became less patient.

Marvin Chandler, newly installed as the plant manager, had the kind of careful voice that made people listen because they couldn't tell whether he was calm or merely empty.

He had not yet learned the place. He was learning it in pieces. A briefing on safety culture. A tour of the turbine deck. A walk past the diesel generator room with someone telling him it was all "well maintained," a phrase that meant nothing without context.

He looked at the weather reports with the concern of a man who had read enough to know he should be concerned but not enough to know what it would cost. In the control room, a Chief Shift Engineer pointed out the storm-related preparations in the same tone he might have used to discuss refueling water chemistry.

"They'll want us at heightened readiness in case we lose offsite power."

"We're not losing offsite power," someone said, not confidently, just reflexively.

The supervisor didn't argue. He didn't need to. He'd been in the industry long enough to know that losing offsite power wasn't something you predicted like an event. It was something you prepared for like a weakness.

Dale was not there to hear any of it. At Silver Ridge, he arrived at a facility that felt familiar in the wrong way. It was combined cycle, not nuclear reactors. Gas turbines coupled to heat recovery steam generators that fed a steam turbine. The same smells of hot insulation and oil and cooling water. The same humming, the same vibration you felt through your shoes when you walked certain sections of grating. Different people. Different politics. Same physics. It was always comforting to him that physics was a universal law holding everyone within its constraints.

He had been assigned quickly, presented as a transfer opportunity. He had signed the paperwork, taken the tour, and nodded at the right moments, but he hadn't stopped thinking about Torlon Hills. You can't empty your heart and soul of a long-term love overnight.

He and Callie went to the Silver Ridge control room and watched the storm forecasts the way they watched risk charts, not as entertainment, but as a map of what would fail first. They could feel it coming. Dale wasn't yet comfortable in this new, non-nuclear environment. Why couldn't the weather just be courteous and let him come to speed on this plant before casting its spell.

Later, in the plant conference room, someone had weather radar up on the screen. The image was still mostly green and yellow. It looked harmless. It didn't look like the kind of thing that rewrote lives. Dale and Callie both knew better. They knew a storm didn't need to look spectacular to be destructive. It just needed to push a system past its margin. They had lived long enough to develop a private distrust of margins that existed only in spreadsheets.

Dale stepped outside and felt the air. It was colder than it should have been for that date. The kind of cold that didn't drift in and drift out. It just hung heavily.

The wind, still light, carried a dampness that wasn't supposed to coexist with that kind of cold. There was no question about it, ice was coming. You could feel it. You could taste it.

He returned inside and asked the Control Operator a simple question.

"How's your black start capability here?"

The operator blinked once, surprised to hear it asked so plainly.

"We're not designated," he said.

"Doesn't matter," Dale replied. "If the grid gets into trouble, everyone becomes part of the story."

That evening, they received another email from the MARES system-wide storm posture update, again written in language designed to be defensible later:

"Expected widespread icing on northern transmission corridors. Sustained winds. Increased likelihood of line trips and generation derates. All black start units should confirm readiness and fuel assurance."

Callie read the sentence twice. All black start units. She stared at the phrase like it might change. She thought again of Franklin. She pictured Teddy's attestation sheets. Clean as paper, confident as lies. She further thought of Samuel Tribetti's quiet statement: We are very good at managing what we can see.

You couldn't see ice until it was already on the conductor. You could see the storm building, though. It developed in numbers, not drama. Pressure was falling. Wind was rising. The bitter cold was holding.

At midnight, the coastal low's central pressure dropped another notch. The models tightened their spread. The track settled into the worst corridor.

The phone at MARES rang more often. The shift turnover briefings grew longer. The operators spoke in shorter phrases. It wasn't panic. It was focus.

At two in the morning, an operator called out, not loudly, just enough for the row to hear.

"Cort 345 trip."

Samuel looked up.

A western feeder into the Hudson corridor had flashed from green to amber to gray. The storm was still offshore. The ice had not yet arrived. But the grid had already started to shed the small things. They were the early, trivial injuries that preceded the serious ones.

"How?" Samuel asked.

"Tree contact," the operator said after checking the alarm details. "Fault cleared. Reclosed. Holding."

Samuel nodded. He didn't feel relieved. By dawn, the wind had shifted east. It came in with a taste of ocean salt and cold iron. The rain began as rain. It had the sound of a normal day.

Then the temperature at the surface held stubbornly at twenty-nine degrees while the air above warmed just enough to melt everything into liquid. The first glaze appeared on handrails.

On the MARES one-line, nothing looked different. Power still flowed. Frequency still hovered at sixty. Tie schedules still matched. Outside, the physical world began collecting weight. Ice did not announce itself. It simply accumulated.

By mid-morning, field crews began reporting visible ice on the northern 345 structures. Not dramatic. A quarter inch. Then half. The kind of ice that made insulators look thicker. The kind of ice that changed the shape of a conductor just enough for wind to start playing with it.

On the operations floor, Samuel watched a line loading value creep upward as generation redispatched around the first trouble spots. The system was doing what it always did, pushing power around failures, leaning harder on what remained.

He thought of the map in his head. He thought of the northern spine. He thought of how much of this region's transfer capability relied on a small number of corridors that looked redundant on paper and behaved like single points in weather.

He watched the atmospheric pressure value in the weather overlay. It was falling faster now. In the afternoon, the wind picked up. Not with a roar, but with stubborn persistence.

Out in the field, a transmission operator reported galloping conductors on the Tannin 230 kV line. Ice-sheathed conductors were moving in slow, wide oscillations as the wind struck them at just the wrong angle.

The galloping wasn't just movement. It was mechanical stress. It was fittings loosening. It was clashing phases. It was the kind of phenomenon that made every line crew's stomach tighten because it wasn't about a single fault; it was about the structure losing its composure.

Samuel watched the oscillation indicator flicker more often. Not severe. Not yet. The grid was still holding. It was still adapting. It was still assuming the next component would do its job.

The operators at Sentinel Creek stood at a window watching ice form on the edge of the maintenance shop roof. Thin at first. Then thick enough to catch light. The mural on the wall, Sentinel Creek winding through painted trees, looked suddenly less like a decorative touch and more like a reminder of how fragile all of this was.

Callie and Dale slipped into Dale's office at Silver Ridge. Callie sat with a cup of coffee and looked at Dale with concern in her eyes.

"What are your thoughts?"

He took another look at the weather radar displayed on his open laptop.

"It's worse than we think."

Even though she wasn't there, she knew Sentinel Creek was as ready as it could be. The grid was not yet broken, but the storm was no longer a forecast. It was now lodging on the conductors. It was icing on the cooling towers. It was in the wind.

At MARES, Samuel stood behind the transmission desk and watched the northern corridor line loadings creep toward limits that existed for a reason. He watched the atmospheric pressure continue to fall. He watched the radar fill in, the colors deepening, the precipitation band tightening like a belt pulled too far.

Someone behind him said, "We're going to lose transmission lines."

Samuel didn't correct him. They all knew. It wasn't a question of "if" anymore. It was a question of order. A question of what would go first. A question of whether they would see it in time.

On the wall, the weather layer refreshed. The storm had a defined center now. The atmospheric pressure number next to it was low enough to feel wrong. Wind arrows clustered around it like insects.

Samuel looked intently at the grid one-line, then at the weather, then back at the grid. He thought, not for the first time, about assumptions. The room remained calm. These men were professionals. They knew what to do. It didn't matter. The storm simply didn't care.

Just before nightfall, the Setab A 500 kV line flashed amber. This time not an oscillation, not a warning, the line tripped. The operator announced with controlled emotion.

"Setab A 500 kV line trip." He looked over at Samuel. "Luckily Torlon Hills Unit 1 is in outage. The north loop is still hanging in there. Flow just slammed onto Setab B and Hudson."

His hand moved to the keyboard. The grid began to shift. Samuel watched the frequency value tremble—59.98… 59.96… then steady.

The room did not panic. It adjusted. Outside, the wind rose another notch. Ice thickened on steel. The storm was not yet at full strength. But it was no longer waiting. It had arrived, and it was just beginning.

***

Part 11

The Breaking Point

****

The wind did not arrive all at once. It strengthened in increments, as if testing the grid before committing to it.

At MARES, the operations floor lights were steady and dim. The wall-sized one-line diagram still showed an interconnected system, though thinner now. Setab A was already out. Setab B was carrying what remained of the northern transfer. Canyon Creek 500 kV had taken more than its share of the burden. The 345 kV corridors were no longer margins. They were structure.

Samuel Tribetti stood behind the transmission desk and watched numbers instead of radar. Wind and ice were atmospheric problems. Loading was a systems problem. Systems problems were predictable, until they weren't.

"Hudson 345 at ninety-six percent," an operator said quietly.

No one reacted. Ninety-six was still less than a hundred.

Outside, the rain had become something else. It fell as liquid, but it didn't remain liquid. Every exposed surface carried a glaze now. Insulators thickened. Crossarms carried weight they had not been asked to carry since installation testing. Field crews in the northern corridor reported heavy radial ice on the Setab structures. Two inches. It did not sound catastrophic. It was. Water weighs about 8.3 pounds a gallon. Water doesn't stick and remain. Ice does.

A dispatcher looked up from a console, raising his voice for the first time.

"Torlon Hills – 2 just relayed offline with a generator step-up transformer sudden pressure."

It was the first strong emotion on the floor in quite some time.

Several minutes later Samuel's direct line rang. The Chief Shift Engineer spoke in a tense, clipped rhythm.

"This is Unit 2 at Torlon Hills. We are scrammed and offline. Our generator step-up transformer has failed. Fire is contained to the transformer enclosure and fire suppression is active. We will be unavailable for the foreseeable future." He paused. "This is not good."

Samuel closed his eyes briefly. He faintly remembered Joel Adamson's maintenance deferral memos that had been long forgotten about the transformers.

"Murphy's Law" he muttered to himself. One more thing to deal with.

Another ten minutes later and the wind shifted fifteen degrees. The Setab B 500 kV line tripped without spectacle. No explosion. No visible flash. A relay action. A line on the one-line mimic turning from red to gray.

"Setab B open," the operator announced.

Samuel did not swear. He did not raise his voice. He looked immediately to Hudson and Cort 345 flows. Hudson surged. Cort followed. Voltage at Palisade sagged, then stabilized.

The grid absorbed the loss the way it had been trained to do, by leaning harder on what remained.

"Dispatch Northwind," Samuel said.

"Already at the limit."

The Lake Coal Plant was down to one unit. Silver Ridge was down to a single 600 MW block. Both units at Torlon Hills were now unavailable. There were no spare megawatts hiding in the corners. The interties with neighboring independent system operators would have to pick up the slack, if they had it to give. Samuel already knew they were probably at their limits anyway.

The next alarm came from the field, not the screen.

"Hudson 345 East reporting conductor wind gallop."

Galloping was not failure. It was a warning. On the structure cameras, the conductors moved in slow, deliberate arcs, the ice having reshaped them into airfoils. The wind found the new geometry and began playing with it. The oscillations were wide, slow, and violent in a way that didn't look violent. Regardless of how gentle it looked, these oscillations could bring down towers.

At 02:14, Hudson 345 tripped. It was on the far western side of the system.

The frequency display dipped — 59.94… 59.88…

Under-frequency relays at Dawkin shed a block of distribution feeders automatically. Lights went out in neighborhoods that had not yet realized they were part of a failing system. Samuel feared this was only the beginning. Much more was to come.

Cort 345 surged in response and only lasted eight minutes. When it went, it went hard due to a phase-to-phase contact caused by clashing conductors under ice load. The relay report would later show it clearly. In the moment, it was simply another line turning gray.

The northern spine was no longer a spine. It was in fragments. Every line action would spin a completely different set of variables. Power that was flowing one direction on a line could immediately reverse and overload going in the opposite direction.

At Redstone Valley nuclear plant, the units saw the instability before anyone spoke it. Turbine governors reacted to frequency swings that were no longer symmetrical. Excitation systems pushed reactive support into a grid that was beginning to separate.

“Voltage collapse at Palisade,” someone said.

Samuel nodded once.

“Begin northern zone undervoltage shedding.”

Load dropped in controlled blocks. Whole communities were going dark. It helped, but only briefly.

Then the Blackstone combined cycle plant tripped. The cold that had pooled against the Appalachians had done its work on the gas infrastructure long before the grid noticed. Gas pressure fell below the combustion control threshold on their gas turbine. The turbine attempted to compensate. It could not.

“Blackstone unit trip.”

Six hundred megawatts vanished in a single line of text.

Frequency dropped sharply now — 59.80… 59.72… 59.65…

Under-frequency load shedding cascaded across Spearville and Dominion. Harbor's distribution feeders opened in segments. Streetlights went dark in widening circles.

The grid was no longer re-dispatching. It was defending.

Canyon Creek 500 kV, now carrying the burden of east-west stability alone, began to oscillate under load and wind simultaneously. Ice had thickened on inland structures. Coastal gusts had pushed farther west than forecast, much farther than anyone believed possible in a single storm.

On a remote structure camera feed, a lattice tower began to lean under asymmetric ice loading. No one on the floor lingered on the image. They watched the numbers.

Canyon Creek rose from 103% to 105%.

"Canyon Creek 500 at emergency limit," the operator said.

Then:

"Canyon Creek open."

The sound in the room did not change. But Samuel knew the system had just crossed the line between disturbance and collapse. Power that had flowed in a loop now had nowhere to go.

Both units at Redstone Valley nuclear plant momentarily over-generated against shrinking load and tripped on protective settings designed for exactly that condition. Two large nuclear plants in an instant were no longer connected to the grid. There were no reserves now. Every loss of power production directly equated to lights going out somewhere on the grid. It was simple math. You cannot take out something you didn't put in.

In the southern island, frequency sagged without northern support. Northwind ramped hard. Silver Ridge held what it could.

At 02:45 Northwind tripped. The audibly rattled operator reported:

“Northwind cooling tower collapsed, unit tripped on condenser backpressure.”

Samuel intercepted the line in disbelief.

“Why did your cooling tower collapse?”

“We are shorthanded. No one was doing ice checks and the fans were all running. Apparently, it internally iced until the structure failed.”

The operators at Torlon Hills were busy doing safe shutdown protocols. They noticed the erratic brightness level of internal lights as the grid suffered failures. For now, offsite power remained at Torlon Hills.

At 03:02, a 345 kV structure on the Hudson corridor failed. The first indication was not the tower. It was the alarms.

"Hudson 345, loss of line. No reclose."

The one-line turned gray. Voltage sagged at Junction Gap. Reactive reserves disappeared faster than the operators could call them up.

A field radio call cut through the internal chatter, clipped and slightly distorted.

"We've got structures down. It's in the right-of-way. The conductors are on the ground."

No elaboration. No emotion. Just fact. The line did not merely trip. It ceased to exist.

At Junction Gap, voltage dropped below recoverable margin. Out-of-step protection activated on the remaining ties. The Atlantic Intertie separated.

The one-line diagram at MARES began turning gray in sections too large to process as events. Frequency fell below 59.3 in the southern island. Under-frequency load shedding relays opened every pre-programmed feeder possible to maintain stability. It was not enough. The system did what systems do when synchronism is lost. It ceased being one.

Generators tripped on protective relays. Transmission lines opened on loss of synchronism. Substations went dark. Lights and heat were failing throughout the service area. Across the MARES region, cities lost power not as a single blackout, but as rolling horizons of failure moving outward from broken corridors.

On the wall-sized display, a few islands remained. These were small pockets of generation holding load, with the electrical frequency hunting high and low as governor controls fought for equilibrium. The governors reacted. The turbines could not.

For a minute, one of those islands looked like it might settle. Then it didn't. The remaining colored segments faded to gray. The frequency display read zero.

For a moment the room was silent. No alarms screamed. No one shouted. The grid had not exploded. It had simply exceeded its margins. For the first time since the network had been built, there was no synchronized generation anywhere in the MARES system.

Outside, the wind continued to rise. It wasn't over yet. In the northern corridor, more structures began to fail under a weight no spreadsheet had ever fully captured.

The phones were ringing steadily. Samuel's face was ashen as he answered his cellphone. It was the Director of the SOC from his home.

"Our nation's capital is in the dark, along with every major city in the northern Atlantic region. Can you give me some kind of recovery estimate?"

Samuel looked at the entirely gray wall.

"We are in full system collapse," he said evenly. "No stable islands. Transmission integrity is compromised. Recovery will require physical reconstruction. And the only way back is black start, and we just lost half the units capable of doing it."

He paused, shaking his head slowly.

"I don't have a timeline."

Dale and Callie were surprised when the lights went out in his office at Silver Ridge. They sprang up and went straight to the control room aided by the battery powered emergency lighting in the admin hallways. They arrived in the control room to watch the two control operators pounding through displays trying to bring the plant to a safe shutdown while numerous alarms squawked loudly in the background.

Dale was out of his element. A lifetime of nuclear had him looking for multiple layers of technical supervision. The fossil side could not be more different. No shift supervisor. No senior operator. Two control room operators and four "outside" or field operators. All this was quite typical for a 1200 MW gas fired combined cycle plant. Callie's plant only had one control operator and two "field" operators per shift.

The Operations Supervisor that Dale inherited with the job was not there. He was dayshift only. Dale had only spent a few minutes with him. He didn't have a clue if he was competent or not.

For the first time since his earliest training days in the Navy, Dale felt frustrated at his lack of knowledge on the process he was now the declared manager. Callie sensed his tension. She leaned closer to him and quietly advised.

"The grid is down. They need to ensure the EEG." She paused to reframe the reference. "The emergency engine generator has started to keep the batteries charged."

She apparently didn't speak quietly enough. One of the control operators quickly responded.

"The EEG started. I have one of my outside operators there now."

Dale looked directly at Callie.

"Jump in. This is far more your comfort area than mine." He gave her a short, reassuring smile. "I am still trying to figure out where the reactor is."

Even in the drama of the moment, she smiled broadly, and then walked closer to the operator.

"Have you opened all of the turbine steam drains?"

"Yes, most of them opened automatically." He was tense and struggling. A complete loss of incoming power was very rare, and always unnerving.

"Close them. Now. All of them."

He looked at her partially confused and partially angry.

"Why?"

"Your vacuum pumps tripped when station service failed. You're dumping high-pressure drain steam into a condenser that can't hold vacuum."

He looked away from Callie and directly at Dale. Dale immediately reacted.

"You heard her. CLOSE your steam drains!"

He looked at the other control room operator for a moment. It was too late. Out in the plant there came a deep, throbbing, boom as steam ripped through the leaded rupture diaphragm on the turbine low pressure hood. It continued venting, reducing heat and energy levels in the condenser.

Callie turned towards Dale shaking her head slowly.

"I think you are screwed. Even if incoming power is restored, you can't restart until the rupture disk is replaced. Do you know if you even have one in the warehouse?"

"No idea." He said with resignation in his voice. "You have spent almost as much time at this plant as I have."

Callie turned back to the two operators on the large console.

"What are your names?"

"I am Geno Timmons, he is Albert Sorenson."

"Geno, Albert, listen carefully. You need to drain the out of service heat recovery steam generators. The unit that just tripped must be bottled-up and then drained when the pressure gets below 10 psig. Anything with water in it is going to freeze." She stepped up to the console. "This is no longer recovery, this is safe shutdown and preserve the plant."

She walked between them, addressing both while looking at the console.

"You need to get your outside operators to purge the hydrogen from the generators. If you lose your EEG, you will lose your hydrogen seal oil pumps when the batteries go dead."

Geno again looked at Dale.

"Do everything she tells you. I can assure you, she knows what she is talking about."

Dale nodded his head at them. He then turned to Callie.

"Callie, you got this. I am going to call Torlon Hills. No one knows that plant any better than I do and I can certainly do more good there, than here."

Callie nodded. Dale walked out into the hall to get away from the alarm horns in the control room so he could better hear the phone.

He had Marvin Chandler's cellphone number. He dialed it. No answer. He tried a couple of other people at Torlon Hills until a call went through to Herman Distel, one of the Ops managers. Dale didn't know him well, but felt he was competent from previous interactions.

"Herman, Dale Morrison here. What's happening at Torlon?"

"It's not good Dale. Our generator step-up transformer on unit - 2 failed. Catastrophically. Fire's out now. We have lost all off-site power. We are on our emergency backup generators and still doing scram and safe shutdown protocols."

A pause. Herman hesitantly continued.

"Did you hear about Marvin Chandler and Jerry Thompson, his senior Ops Manager?"

"No, I haven't talked to anyone."

"They called from Marvin's company pickup truck and said they broke down on the way to the plant and asked if we could send someone to get them." He paused.

"Apparently right after that someone slid off the ice-packed road and hit them. Hard."

"Are they okay?" Dale asked quickly.

"I heard they were hurt pretty bad, but no news beyond that."

Dale shook his head.

"When it rains, it pours."

"What's that?" Herman asked.

"Just something my Dad always said. Never mind. Are the diesels behaving?" Dale knew everything was riding on the emergency diesels now.

"B-train's… Hunting a little."

Dale didn't like the way he said it.

"Fuel pressure?"

"Fluctuating. We're seeing a temperature drop on the return leg. There were some heat trace alarms earlier tonight. It got logged."

"Was it fixed?"

Silence.

"It wasn't prioritized."

"Any idea what is happening on the grid?"

"The Chief Shift Engineer just reached the MARES SOC." He paused. "You are not going to believe this, but they are on their emergency diesels." He paused again to let that take hold. "The grid has completely collapsed. They told him there are multiple 500 and 345 kV towers laying on the ground from ice. We are going to be without incoming station service for a while." There was some noise in the background. He paused. "No offense Dale, but I have a reactor to keep cool. I have to go."

Dale stepped out into the parking lot and stopped. The wind was not howling. It pressed, steady and relentless. A chill ran down his back. Not from the cold so much as the surreal view from the parking lot.

The entire facility had been transformed into something unrecognizable. Every truck in the lot was encased in clear armor. Mirrors drooped under the weight of the ice. Antennas were bent into shallow arcs. The security fence shimmered like decorative glass.

The parking lot light poles, now dark, wore thick sleeves of ice like a child's jacket that was too large. The asphalt beneath his boots was not asphalt anymore. It was a single, continuous sheet of sheer ice. He attempted to walk a few careful steps forward. This was not going to happen. He knew he couldn't stay upright.

The air carried a low, constant howl. It wasn't thunder or machinery. It was more a composite noise. It was wind blowing through iced lattice along the fence line. There were distant cracks as branches surrendered.

Across the access road, a row of distribution feeders sagged visibly, their geometry altered. They were still intact. For now, anyway.

He looked upward. The transmission structures that fed Silver Ridge stood in profile against a steel sky, their lattice frames thickened, distorted by frozen weight. The conductors were no longer round lines. They were elongated, sculpted shapes, sagging lower than they should.

He pulled his phone from his pocket. One bar. He opened a weather app out of habit. It struggled to load. Finally, a radar image appeared. It clearly revealed bands wrapping tight around a dark center offshore. The central pressure reading blinked and refreshed lower.

The storm was intensifying. He thought of the nation's capital, and the cities and homes affected by what he was witnessing. Inside those homes, thermostats were clicking uselessly. Ovens had been opened for heat. Flashlights were being hunted in drawers. Children asking when the lights were coming back on, wrapped in blankets. People were probably annoyed, but not afraid. Not yet anyway.

In the row-houses and suburban cul-de-sacs, neighbors stood at windows watching ice accumulate on tree limbs and assuming utility crews were already mobilized. They expected inconvenience. Hours. Maybe until morning if it were really bad. They did not understand that if steel towers were folding in transmission system rights-of-way, power could be days or more away. They did not understand that when a lattice structure collapses under ice load, it does not simply get restrung. It requires rebuilding. Component availability, heavy equipment, intensive labor. Rebuilding even one transmission tower took time. Maybe hundreds? He shuddered.

They also did not understand that access roads were impassable. That cranes could not travel on glazed ice. That line crews could not climb towers that no longer stood.

At large chain grocery stores, generators hummed behind buildings, preserving inventory for now. In hospitals, automatic transfer switches had engaged. Diesel engines were running. However, diesel fuel is finite. Most fuel tanks were sized for hours, not days.

In high-rise apartment buildings, elevators had stopped between floors. Water pressure would follow within hours when rooftop tanks emptied. Emergency crews would respond to stalled elevators as fast as they could. For now, they had other, more critical emergencies. Vehicle crashes from ice. Most were slow, grinding crashes but injuries were still present. Airbags injuring people in what was considered the lesser of two evils. Traffic lights were dark. Intersections were already becoming negotiation points.

Dale looked again at the transmission structures. One of them moved, not dramatically, not collapsing, just a subtle deflection under a gust that came stronger than the last. The ice was redistributing.

Dale closed his eyes for a moment. This was no longer about megawatts. It was about days, even possibly weeks in some corridors. He carefully turned back toward the admin entrance. His feet slipped out from under him. He was on the ground in an instant. Nothing was broken. It just hurt. The ice didn't even notice when he hit.

Dale struggled to get back on his feet due to the layer of ice on everything he touched. The plant condition was spinning through his thoughts. The big thing was time. Thirty minutes without station service was an inconvenience. Thirty hours was stress. Seventy-two hours was damage. A week or more was societal.

Inside, Callie was stabilizing a plant that might not restart for days if that rupture disk was not in stock. At Torlon, Herman was listening to diesel engines whose reliability curve narrowed with every passing hour. At MARES, Samuel was stunned, staring at a gray wall while trying to design a resurrection without an intact transmission system.

Dale opened the door and stepped back into emergency-lit corridors of Silver Ridge. Behind him, the wind strengthened another notch. He entered the control room. Callie was sitting on the edge of the control room operator's desk monitoring the operator's safe shutdown progress. He quietly placed his hand on her shoulder.

"Follow me."

She walked with him to the admin building entrance. As she exited the door, the otherworldly appearance of the plant surroundings caused her to miss a breath. She took in the devastation and slowly turned and looked at Dale with shock on her face.

"I've never seen anything this bad before."

"Neither have I." He said quietly, taking her hand into his.

"My parents…" She trailed off. "I must call my parents and warn them this is serious."

Across the region, millions of people were waiting for a flicker that was not coming. Not tonight. Maybe not for days. This one was going down in the history books.

As they returned to the control room, the desk phone rang and Geno picked it up.

"Silver Ridge Control Room."

"Yes he is. Just a moment."

Geno motioned to Dale.

"It's for you."

Dale took the receiver.

"Dale Morrison."

It was Cal Johnson. VP of nuclear. Dale's former boss.

"Dale, I figured I would find you there. We have a serious issue I need your help with."

"What's that?" Dale asked, honestly not sure where this was leading.

"Marvin Chandler and Jerry Thompson were in a serious accident on their way to the plant tonight."

He lowered his voice.

"I don't have any details, but I know it is serious."

He cleared his throat and continued.

"I have been talking to the plant people and they are all saying, call Dale."

Dale had a momentary flash of anger.

"What are you asking, Cal?"

"I need you to get to Torlon Hills as soon as possible. I know they have major issues and the NRC is going to be all over this one. I need your expertise there, now."

Dale's anger flared again.

"Are you certain you want to send in second string right now?"

"Dale, I am told you are as technically qualified as anyone could be. Can we put this behind us right now and you go back to Torlon and do your magic?"

"I will leave now."

***

Part 12

The Long Night

****

The wind had not stopped, but it had lost its violence. It no longer attacked. It simply persisted.

By dawn the precipitation tapered to mist and then nothing at all. The sky lightened from iron gray to a thin washed blue that felt inappropriate above what lay beneath it. Temperatures dropped quickly as the low pulled away. Fifteen degrees. Then twelve. The ice did not melt. It simply hardened.

***

MARES SOC

At MARES, the operations floor looked unchanged except for one detail. The wall-sized one-line diagram remained entirely gray.

Samuel Tribetti stopped answering the continuous phone calls. He had no answers. The system had not changed. The difference was not activity. It was the total absence of activity. No power flows. No frequency oscillations. No tie schedules. Just dead topology.

"Any stable islands?" someone asked quietly.

"Negative," the transmission desk replied. "We've confirmed structural loss on Hudson West, Hudson East, Cort, and at least two 500 kV spans on Setab. Field reports say Canyon Creek has a conductor on the ground near mile marker forty-three. Access roads are impassable."

"How many towers?"

"Unknown."

Unknown was worse than a number.

Samuel leaned forward.

"Switch to physical damage assessment protocol," he said. "Assume extended outage."

No one argued.

Samuel Tribetti had started in a Department of Energy dispatch center more than twenty years earlier. He had moved steadily through three private utilities before accepting the MARES supervisor role. Coming to Mares brought him back to his boyhood home. His wife was pleased to be back near her family.

Nothing in those years had prepared him for a silent grid. Telemetry control was gone. Worse, the primary SOC was without incoming power. Two backup diesel generators kept the building lit and barely warm. The SOC rode on its own emergency generation for the first time ever. Unfortunately, diesel fuel tanks were finite. Samuel made the call to Guy Richardson, the backup SOC supervisor in Ohio. Samuel did not leave his chair.

"Guy," he said into the secure line. "We are transferring operational control to you."

In the hardened secondary control facility in Ohio, Guy Richardson had been watching the same gray one-line for hours. The site was minimally staffed, as designed. Two transmission operators. One communications technician. Redundant servers humming behind reinforced walls.

"We're ready," Guy replied.

The transfer protocol was formal and deliberate. Authority flags shifted within the Energy Management System. Control tags reassigned. Telemetry routing confirmed. Primary dispatch permissions locked out. Secondary permissions enabled.

Ohio now held the controls.

Samuel remained in the darkened primary SOC, its lighting reduced to conserve diesel fuel. He was no longer dispatching the grid. He was coordinating its survival.

“Confirm you have supervisory control,” Samuel said.

“Confirmed,” Guy replied. “Primary EMS is now shadow only. We have command authority.”

Samuel nodded, though Guy could not see him.

“Understood. We will handle triage and field coordination from here.”

Control had moved. Leadership had not. The recovery, no matter how labored, would be directed from this now, virtually dark facility.

When the primary SOC dimmed into emergency lighting, it felt symbolic, though it was not. It was prudent planning. For the first time in its operating history, MARES was running from its hardened secondary facility in Ohio. They were managing a grid that did not currently exist.

Samuel shifted to triage. Ohio was handling the controls. He would set priorities. Hospitals, critical communications, water treatment, natural gas compressor stations, and fuel distribution centers. It then hit him like a hammer. Torlon Hills, and Redstone Valley nuclear plants. Decay heat does not stop because the turbines do. He had to prioritize station power back to them, first. He immediately reordered the list. Torlon Hills, Redstone Valley, hospitals. Communications, gas compressor stations, and fuel.

Transmission damage assessment would be ongoing. Restoration would follow reconstruction, not switching. He began making calls to adjoining service areas for any help they could provide. MidAtlantic was not recovering from this without outside help.

***

Torlon Hills Nuclear Plant

At Torlon Hills, the reactor sat subcritical and cooling. Steam generators were stable, and decay heat was manageable. For now, anyway.

A-train diesel held steady.

B-train continued to hunt erratically.

Fuel oil temperature at the return header was still dropping. Herman Distel stood near the diesel control panel while an operator traced the heat trace circuit with a flashlight and handheld multimeter.

"Breaker's closed," the operator said.

"Then why's it cold?" Herman asked.

Silence.

Wind-driven ice had worked into places it was never meant to reach. Heat tracing that had functioned for years had lost integrity somewhere along a run no one had physically inspected in months.

Fuel oil does not forgive cold. It thickens quietly. The return line temperature had fallen below the cloud point. The fuel was beginning to gel.

The diesels were over-designed to be robust. The fuel system was the weak link in the chain. If the fuel gelled, the B-train would not last.

Herman immediately began making calls for portable generators and temporary heat. The NRC would expect it, and the plant required it. The total loss of decay heat removal was unthinkable.

The Generator Step-Up Transformer (GSU) for unit – 2 was destroyed. Kendall Allen finally reached Dale, who had been called back to Torlon by Cal Johnson.

"Dale, this is Kendall Allen. We need to know the status of the unit – 2 GSU."

Dale did not try and soften the blow.

"It appears to be a total loss. As near as I can tell looking at the trends, when Setab – B tripped, the VAR loading shifted radically. The transformer incurred the reactive shift and probably arced internally and picked up the sudden pressure relay. The generated acetylene and hydrogen combusted."

Kendall rubbed his neck and shook his head.

"How much collateral damage besides the transformer?"

"The fire was semi contained, in the enclosure. A company pickup parked near the transformer was destroyed but thank God no one was hurt. Anyway, the fire suppression systems engaged and eventually extinguished the flames."

Kendall didn't have any further questions. He knew this was far from over.

***

Silver Ridge

Callie stabilized what she could. While doing so she added depth to the Silver Ridge operators' understanding. Their respect for her was increasing by the hour.

The rupture disk had blown with a sound that would stay with her. Condenser vacuum could never be reestablished until physical replacement of the blown rupture disk. Without vacuum in the condenser, the plant would remain inoperable.

She moved through the plant deliberately, instructing operators on essentials like bottling the heat recovery steam generators and preparing for an extended shutdown. As she roamed the plant she found that one of the huge circulating water pump circuit breakers were still closed. She called for the operator to come to the breaker cubicle.

“Sorry it took some time to get here.” The operator was out of breath and still partially disheveled by the loss of all incoming power.

Callie knew he was struggling with everything.

“See this 4160 Volt circuit breaker for that huge circulating water pump?”

“Yes.”

"Do you notice what position it is in?"

The operator looked at the mechanical indicator on the door of the cabinet.

"It says it's closed?"

Callie shook her head yes.

"When this load center is reenergized, it would power up that circ water pump. I am guessing the discharge valve is still open on the pump. If this happened, it could send a massive water hammer and do extensive damage to the circulating water piping and the condenser. It is imperative that you check ALL the large circuit breakers to ensure they opened as they were supposed to."

He looked at her with deep concern.

"Thank you so much for this. I had no idea. I figured all the large circuit breakers would have opened automatically."

Callie touched his arm.

"They were supposed to. Never assume anything under these conditions."

They walked through the rest of the circuit breakers together. When they were done Callie explained the next big task to prepare for a possible long-term shutdown.

"You must vent the hydrogen off the generators in a controlled fashion. This is to prevent it from gushing through the seals if the emergency seal oil pump fails."

He thanked her again. She returned to the control room to ensure they understood the sequence necessary to bring the plant into safe shutdown status.

She instructed them to secure all rotating equipment. Maintain lubrication and cooling while power was available. Prepare for the possibility that it would not be. The plant could not restart. It could only be preserved.

***

Blackstone Generating Station

Lance Armor, the plant manager of Blackstone was contacted by Anthony Newson, the VP of fossil generation. He was quite upset at the report he received.

"Lance, can you shed some light on what happened to your cooling tower?"

"Yes sir. As you know, the cooling towers are constructed of wood and fiberglass. Because of the employee turnover I was one operator short on shift last night."

He paused to ensure Anthony fully grasped his understaffing issue before continuing.

"Larry Austin, the control room operator is new to the job. He is a decent kid, but was clueless that leaving all twelve fans on high speed would cause icing inside the tower structure during conditions we had last night. The outside operator was busy inside because of the missing operator. No one noticed the extreme icing inside the tower. It apparently built-up to the point where the weight overcame the structure. It is a total loss. We will be down for months rebuilding the tower."

Anthony's tone remained flat.

"We will, of course, conduct a full root cause analysis."

***

The Public – Morning One

Morning came without alarm clocks. People woke up because they were cold. Thermostats had clicked uselessly through the night. Homes built for convenience began to lose stored heat. Interior temperatures fell into the fifties. Then forties. Children were gleefully showing their parents that they could "see their breath."

Oven doors were opened and gas ranges burned longer than they should. Fireplaces were lit in homes that had not used them in years.

In high-rises, water pumps had already failed. The upper floors lost pressure first and the toilets stopped flushing as the faucets ran dry.

Cell service weakened as backup batteries drained. Some tower sites had generators. Many did not.

Traffic lights remained dark. Police moved to manual intersection control where they could. Ice still coated the roads. Braking was virtually impossible. For those that still had cell service, images and videos of slow-moving cars sliding aimlessly into curbs and other cars were everywhere. All outdoor movement was slow and uncertain.

Hospitals were running, for now anyway. Diesel generators throbbed steadily and fuel suppliers were contacted. Delivery trucks were stuck, unable to negotiate the layer of ice on every roadway.

Grocery stores opened briefly until generator fuel levels forced conservative shutdown. Gas stations could not pump without power.

The public did not panic. They expected repair trucks. They expected progress. They did not yet understand that transmission towers lay folded across frozen rights-of-way. They were yet to grasp the full extent of the loss.

***

MARES – Midday Assessment

By noon, helicopters finally began reaching the transmission corridors.

Setab corridor: Five collapsed structures confirmed.

Hudson East: Four collapsed structures.

Hudson West: Structural deformation on two spans. Towers still standing.

Canyon Creek: One total collapse. Adjacent towers compromised. Conductors on the ground for miles.

Ford: Four collapsed structures.

Ice depth remained over two inches on many structures. Temperatures were falling toward single digits. Field reconnaissance was ongoing.

Samuel gathered the core operators in the shutdown SOC. He was exhausted, running on adrenaline. His hands shook badly. His mind did not.

"We are not restoring transmission today," he said.

Silence.

"We focus on critical facilities first. Nuclear station service. Hospitals. Water treatment. Black start sequencing once structural integrity is known."

He looked around the room.

"This is no longer a dispatch problem. It's a construction problem."

***

The Psychological Shift

That afternoon the sky cleared. Sunlight struck the ice and turned the region almost beautiful. The beauty felt almost cruel.

News helicopters captured aerial images of towers folded like paper. The images circulated quickly. Concern shifted to frustration. Frustration moved toward fear. Reality was beginning to hit. The politicians already knew that after fear comes panic.

***

Callie

Callie had not told her parents she was helping Dale move into his apartment. She had planned to surprise them later. The storm was everyone's surprise.

Cell service had now failed. She used the landline in the Silver Ridge control room to call her childhood home and check on her parents.

"Hello?" her mother said pensively.

"Mom, it's Callie. Are you and Dad okay?"

"The house is cold, but we're by the fireplace." A pause. "Where are you?"

"I'm about sixty miles away."

She let them assume she was on the road.

"Please be careful driving, sweetie," her mother paused. "When do you think you'll be here?"

"I don't know yet. This power outage will last longer than most people expect. Fill as many water jugs as you can. Dad should drain what piping he can reach. You may lose use of the bathrooms."

"My God, Callie. How bad is it?"

"There's significant transmission damage. I'll explain more later."

"All right, sweetheart."

"Mom… I love you and dad. I'll get there as soon as I can."

She lowered the receiver slowly. Guilt settled in before the phone receiver hit the cradle.

***

Dale

By late afternoon, Dale stood again at his former plant, Torlon Hills. His trip there was slow and labored. He was ever conscious of Marvin's fate. He instinctively parked in the Plant Manager's spot he had used for years without giving it any thought.

Exiting the pickup, he was surprised how steady the wind was. The temperature had dropped ten degrees since he left Silver Ridge.

He did not think about megawatts. This was a battle of duration. Systems without power were already failing. Water. Sanitation. Fuel. Supply chains.

He checked his phone.

No signal.

He looked back south toward the Silver Ridge plant, beyond miles of frozen transmission corridors. The storm had passed. The grid had not. The real work, slow and physical, was just beginning.

***

Part 13

24 Hours After the Collapse

****

MARES – Primary and Secondary SOC

With the secondary SOC fully in command, triage narrowed to execution. The news was uneven. The western portion of MARES had held more structure than the east. The eastern corridors were seriously damaged. Fractured was probably a more appropriate description.

From the secondary SOC facility in Ohio, operators closed the Lignite Intertie and energized the Lignite Substation from the Northern Area Independent System Operator (NAISO) side. The Hudson 345 kV line, though scarred, was serviceable after emergency repairs to damaged bushings and hardware. Crews generously loaned from neighboring NAISO had bravely climbed iced steel before daylight.

Hudson's energization restored offsite power to Redstone Valley Nuclear. Their emergency diesels returned to standby. A badly needed victory.

Torlon Hills would not be near that simple.

At Sentinel Creek, Callie's operators closed the Talon 230 kV line and energized the Dominion Substation using their black-start station diesels. Two distribution feeders came alive. Two medium-sized hospitals and several hundred homes regained electricity. While it may have been small in scale, it carried a significant moral victory.

Thirty-five hours into the event, Samuel Tribetti finally stopped. His body demanded what his mind had resisted until now. He left Guy Richardson in command at the secondary SOC and stepped away from the floor.

***

Field Operations / Eastern Region

Across the eastern corridors, restoration crews were discovering just how much steel the storm had taken.

Restoration was no longer theoretical. It was a basic logistical nightmare.

Lewis Amboy was the lead lineman for the eastern division of MidAtlantic Energy. He was surveying the Hudson East 345 kV line. He called Shane Hollowell who was put in charge of the eastern area repairs.

“Shane, Lewis Amboy here with a status update.”

“I was hoping to hear from you, Lewis. Where are you, and what are you seeing?”

The phone lost signal. He redialed him.

“Shane, are you there?”

It was strobing slightly but he was able to answer.

“I am here Lewis, what do you have for me?”

“It’s pretty bad, Shane. I am at tower 52 on the access road for the Hudson East 345 kV line. Towers 48 through 51 are on the ground. Towers 52 and 53 are severely compromised. The conductors are on the ground for over three miles. I have never seen it this bad.”

"What about alternate paths to Harbor? Any status?"

Lewis looked at his scribbled notes on a filthy clipboard.

"Spearville to Dominion 230 kV has some bushing damage, but not terrible. Cornell from Dominion to Blackstone also has damage, but as far as I know, no towers are down."

It was difficult for Shane to hear him with the wind and the cellphone cutting in and out. Shane raised his voice.

"What about the Ruan 230 kV line?"

"What's that?" Lewis could barely hear him.

"Ruan, the Ruan 230 kV line. What's the status of Ruan?"

"I am told there is one tower down, or badly damaged. I have not seen it myself."

Shane didn't have to think about it. The choice was obvious. They did not have enough structural steel for the 345 kV towers.

"Lewis, focus on Ruan or Canvoy. We need to get a path back into Harbor Substation."

"Roger that, Shane. We will focus on the Ruan, Canvoy, and Cornell 230 kV lines."

"Thanks, Lewis. Let me know if you run into more damage than you expected."

Lewis was 48 years old. Old, for a lineman. The job is hard on your body. He had been through many bouts of tornado damage, and too many bouts with ice damage. This was by far the worst he had ever seen. He knew he couldn't keep this up. Line work was for a younger generation.

***

Torlon Hills Nuclear

Dale immediately followed the NRC guidelines. The required notifications triggered controlled urgency. Portable generators were requested as supplemental insurance for the emergency diesel trains maintaining decay heat removal.

Diesel Train B had been struggling. It finally failed. A breaker feeding a heat-trace panel arced and burned. The fire was small but sufficient. Heat tracing was lost along the entire return fuel-oil leg. Suction temperature dropped rapidly. The fuel gelled. The engine shut down on loss of fuel. The now excruciating cold was exacting a toll on more than just the general public.

Train A now carried the full load alone. The operators did not catch it immediately, but when the Train A diesel doubled its load after Train B failed, something broke internally. Water and glycol coolant began leaking into the engine crankcase. Glycol does not lubricate.

Dale was back at the plant and, for now, in charge. He understood that transmission reconstruction would be deliberate. Junction Gap Substation had to be energized from Franklin if Torlon was going to regain station service in any reasonable time period.

He began making calls. Kendall Allen answered on the second ring.

"Kendall Allen here."

"Kendall, Dale Morrison. I'm at Torlon Hills."

"I just heard. I'm sorry about Marvin."

"Me too." He wasted no time. "I need the Franklin 500 kV line prioritized."

There was a pause.

"D.C. is still mostly dark," Kendall said. "Most of our resources are staged toward getting full capability back into Harbor Substation."

"I realize Harbor is important," Dale replied evenly. "But Torlon Hills is critical. If we lose our decay heat removal margin, the consequences extend well beyond this region. Franklin is the shortest viable path to station service. I need it moved to the top."

"Isn't that why you have the extensive backup diesel network at the plant? Don't forget, I worked nuclear for over three years."

Dale closed his eyes and unconsciously shook his head as his mind replayed, three years.

"Kendall, we've already lost one diesel train due to the intense cold."

Another pause. Calculating, not emotional.

"I'll redirect additional crews," Kendall said. "Franklin moves up."

"Thank you."

The call ended.

***

MidAtlantic Headquarters. Kendall Allen's Office

Kendall called Garrin Storz into his office.

"Garrin, we must reprioritize. We must put everything we have on getting the Franklin 500 kV line to Junction Gap substation, and then onto Torlon Hills. It is now the top priority. We have a nuclear plant existing on one back-up diesel."

"Holy crap! How did we end up with Torlon Hills on one diesel?"

Kendall rolled his eyes.

"I don't have a clue. I just talked to Dale Morrison and he is beside himself on this one."

Garrin looked surprised.

"I heard Dale was moved out of Torlon and put at Silver Ridge."

"Long story. Marvin was just in an accident. Dale is temporarily back. All I know is we must get power back to Torlon as soon as possible. Shift all your resources to the Torlon and Franklin 500 kV lines."

Garrin thought for a moment. The grid topology was firmly implanted in his mind.

"We have the Torlon 500 kV and 345 kV lines between Torlon and the Junction Gap substation. We should choose the easiest line to repair, whichever one that may be, correct?"

"Absolutely. As soon as you get the status for both those lines, pick the quickest."

Garrin made several calls to the line crews doing grid reconnaissance. It was obvious that the Torlon 500 kV line was in better shape. It had been "hardened" due to NRC pressure on MidAtlantic Energy a few years back. The 345 kV line had not. There were five towers down on the 345 kV line. Only one of the "hardened" towers on the 500 kV line was severely damaged.

Garrin reprioritized the line crews to focus on getting station service back into Torlon Hills.

***

Torlon Hills

After talking to Kendall Allen, Dale immediately called Silver Ridge. Callie answered. She had not left the control room in several hours.

"I need a favor," he said.

"Name it."

"I think it is imperative that you travel to Franklin. We need the Twin-Pac lit and one gas turbine online. Not for load, but for our station service. We're now carrying our reactor cooling load on one diesel, and the cold is taking its toll. It is essential we get something lined up ASAP."

There was no hesitation in her voice.

"Will Franklin even let me through the gate?"

"I'll make sure of it."

A brief silence.

"Dale, you know I will do everything I can."

"Be careful getting there," he said.

"Thanks. Keep me posted on your status." She paused before continuing hesitantly. "I appreciate your confidence. I hope this works."

She hung up and began preparing to leave. As she entered the parking lot, she looked at her phone. She had two bars. She immediately dialed her parents.

"Mom, Dad, I cannot come to your house yet. I am helping to get power back on. Are you doing okay?"

They sounded tired, stressed.

"Callie, honey, the only heat is the fireplace. We are bundled up by it, but we still have some wood left." She paused and lowered her voice. “Dad says the pipes and bathroom will freeze if the power isn’t back soon.”

“I’m doing everything I can. Please forgive me for not being there right now.”

“We’re fine. Really. Do what you do, sweetie. It will help everyone.”

They hung up. Guilt twisted in her gut as she carefully slid the car out of the Silver Ridge parking lot.

***

Field Operations / Eastern Region

Shane Hollowell was coordinating with Garrin Storz on triage and reconstruction efforts. An hour and 43 minutes after speaking to Lewis Amboy, Shane’s phone rang. It was Dave Carter. He was another lineman supervisor who worked alongside Lewis Amboy.

“Shane, Dave Carter here. I have some bad news, extremely bad news.”

“What is it Dave?” He expected to hear of more damage. He didn’t expect to hear this.

"Lewis Amboy is dead. He was inspecting a tower when an iced cross arm fell. He couldn't get out of the way fast enough."

Shane was stunned. He took the phone from his ear and turned to Garrin.

"Lewis Amboy was just killed by debris falling from a tower."

Shane put his phone on speaker mode.

"Where is Lewis now?"

"Shane, we did all we could. We tried CPR for several minutes. His injuries…"

Silence.

"His injuries were too extensive."

"Where is he now?"

"We are all still here. We have called a helicopter."

Shane looked at Garrin.

"Dave, this is Garrin Storz. Do not speak to anyone about this yet. We will call his family from this office." He paused. “Dave, I am so sorry. Are you able to keep working?”

There was a long silence. They could hear the wind through the cell phone speaker.

“We’ll do the best we can after the helicopter gets here.”

Garrin immediately called Kendall Allen and told him to alert the corporate legal department. Garrin then volunteered to call Lewis’s family. He had never had to make a call like this before. He was dreading it.

***

Franklin Generating Station

Callie’s trek to Franklin was difficult due to the extreme conditions. The eighty-mile trip took almost four hours. She arrived at the Franklin security gate exhausted from the drive. She pushed the button on the intercom. It took several tries.

“Can I help you?” Finally came the static-laced reply.

“Callie McGraw. I should have clearance to enter.”

There was a several-minute wait. She reached for her phone to call Dale when the gate finally rattled spastically open as it shed ice onto the roadway. There were only three cars in the parking lot. She could faintly hear the two emergency diesels droning in the background. The lights in the parking lot were dark. She pushed the button and buzzed into the control room.

“Is Teddy Warnick here?”

The operator was Don Garcia. He looked at her with a high degree of disinterest.

“He is not here, neither is Eric Royden. Mike Cummings is on his way, but I don’t know when he will arrive.”

He reached over and acknowledged an alarm that flashed on the large overhead alarm display.

“We’re dead in the water. Each block’s on its emergency diesel for lighting and lube oil.”

She tried not to show her annoyance.

"The whole power system is dead. That's why I am here. We need to get the Twin-Pac running as soon as possible."

"Good luck with that piece of shit."

She was surprised at his candor.

"The last time I was here, a gentleman named Alex Cordon was here. He seemed to know something about the unit. Is he here by any chance?"

"Well, he's assigned to this shift," came the dry, sarcastic reply. "He could be anywhere."

"Can you page him or get him on your radio?"

Callie was losing patience. She struggled with bad attitudes, especially when she was exhausted. Don keyed the microphone held loosely in his hand.

"Alex Cordon, Alex Cordon, come to the control room for a visitor." He then looked at Callie. "You just as well have a seat. I have no idea where he is."

Callie then called Dale. She put her phone on speaker mode so Don could hear.

"Dale, this is Callie. I am here at Franklin with the control operator. I am waiting for someone to accompany me to the Twin-Pac. How are things holding there?"

"Not good at all," came the strained reply. "We have torpedo heaters all around the diesels and the fuel tanks, and they are rewiring the heat-trace panel right now. The problem is, when Train A diesel ramped after Train B went down, we picked up an internal coolant leak. We are blowing emulsified oil out of every vent on the engine. Callie, Train A diesel is in death throes right now." He paused. Callie could hear the strain in his voice. "Train B still does not have fuel feed. I have everyone on it."

Dale took his mouth from the phone and hollered at someone near him. Callie could hear intense activity in the background.

"Sorry, Callie. We are taking extraordinary measures to keep Train A diesel running. We need power from Franklin, now!"

"Dale, it is a ghost town here."

Dale's ire rose.

"Teddy knows how critical this Twin-Pac issue is. He was supposed to be there along with his maintenance and ops managers."

Dale paused to compose himself.

"Callie, I will make some more phone calls. I will get back to you."

He hung up. Don Garcia looked at Callie with a suppressed sarcastic grin.

"It's really icy out there. That's probably slowing them down."

Callie's impatience took control.

"Could I use your radio?" she said, reaching out to him.

He handed her the microphone.

"Alex Cordon, Alex Cordon, this is Callie McGraw. I am in the control room. I need you here as soon as possible." She released the transmit button for a moment and then pressed it again, this time raising her voice. "Please acknowledge now."

Silence.

Her phone rang. It was Dale.

"Callie, I guess Eric Royden, Mike Cummings, and Teddy are all in transit and will be there shortly. I can assure you, they know the urgency of this situation."

"Thanks, Dale. I will keep you up to date."

Dale's voice took on an even more serious tone.

"Callie, I cannot impress on you just how critical the need is. The report from the diesel generator room is not encouraging. They are draining emulsified oil from the crankcase and adding new oil continuously. They think it is a cylinder liner or head gasket."

He lowered his voice.

"God help us if Train A diesel seizes or fails."

"I understand."

She hung up.

A few minutes later the door opened to the control room. It was Alex Cordon.

"Sorry for the delay. I was at the water treatment plant. I guess you want to go to the Twin-Pac?"

"Alex, it is critical that we get it running. Is there an operator that can come with us to start it?"

Alex looked at Don.

"Can Liz come to the Twin-Pac with us after Teddy, Mike, and Eric arrive?"

Callie did a double take. Her anger spiked.

"Alex, we need to get to the Twin-Pac now. We can't afford to wait for Teddy and the others. I don't think you realize how critical this situation is!"

"Oh, I understand. But we have been told we must wait for the others to arrive. I don't have permission to take you there until they get here."

Her anger welled. She decided to call Dale again, but just then the control-room door opened. It was Mike

Cummings, the Ops Manager. She did not wait for explanations.

"Mike, we have a rapidly developing issue at Torlon Hills. We must energize the Franklin 500 kV line and the Junction Gap Substation as soon as possible!"

"Cool your jets, Callie. Let me grab a cup of coffee. It is damn cold out there."

Callie's anger was off the chart. She had dealt all too often with this type of dismissive attitude. He apparently did not understand what was at stake.

While Mike was getting his coffee, Eric Royden, the Maintenance Manager, and Teddy Warnick entered the control room stamping the ice and snow from their feet and rubbing their hands.

Callie's pent-up anger boiled over.

"Do the three of you have any idea what is at stake here?"

Teddy erupted.

"Of course we know. We're here to get the Twin-Pac in service. The question is, what are you doing here? You don't have authority at this plant."

Through her anger, Callie knew one of them had to act like the adult. She swallowed her pride and suppressed her anger.

"Teddy, I am here to assist. I am acting as a resource to you and this plant. I have studied our black-start situation carefully. We must get the Twin-Pac running now. As I just told Mike, we must energize the Franklin 500 kV line and the Junction Gap Substation as soon as possible."

Eric Royden, the maintenance manager, raised his voice.

"We can't do this with the Twin-Pac. We will have to spin up the Twin-Pac and energize our switchyard and then use the Twin-Pac to power up one of our GTs. This is the only way to energize the Franklin 500 kV line."

Callie shook her head.

"We don't have time to do all this. I am in touch with Dale Morrison. Their situation is deteriorating rapidly. We must get the Twin-Pac up and use it to energize the Franklin 500 kV line."

Mike looked angrily at Callie while shaking his head.

"I'm telling you, it's never gonna happen, Callie."

He then turned away from her and addressed Teddy directly.

"Teddy, that 40 MW Twin-Pac won't energize our 500 kV transformer and the Franklin 500 kV line. If it does, it won't be able to handle Torlon's reactor feed pumps. I am certain of this."

Teddy looked at Callie.

"I have to agree with Mike and Eric. I don't think it can be done. We need to bring up one of the main gas turbines."

"How long will that take?" Callie asked, knowing well it would require preparing the heat recovery steam generators and the entire steam system. She knew the main gas turbines could not bypass the HRSGs at Franklin. Because of this, they would be required to do the full system lineup, potentially taking hours in their current state.

Mike Cummings, the Operations Manager, jumped back in.

"At least a couple of hours, and that's after we get the Twin-Pac spinning."

Callie knew she must do something.

Eric, Mike, and Teddy looked at each other dismissively and then at Callie. Teddy answered first.

"Callie, I am sorry, but we don't unilaterally do anything of this magnitude without going through the required chain of command. You should know this as a plant manager in MidAtlantic."

"We don't have time to do this. I thought you understood the gravity of this situation?"

"Callie, you don't understand the gravity of what we are dealing with. The transmission and line department has total authority and say on these lines and transformers, especially the 500 kV system!" He looked at Eric and Mike. "See if you can reach anyone in the T&D group. I refuse to move forward without their involvement."

At that moment, Callie felt helpless. She could not force this more than she already had. She said a little prayer under her breath.

"Lord help us."

Eric was unable to reach the first three people on his list. Callie watched the clock tick. Her discomfort was multiplying. Finally, Eric reached Shane Hollowell. He put the phone on speaker so everyone could hear.

"Shane, this is Eric Royden, the maintenance manager at Franklin Energy Center. I am here with Teddy Warnick, Mike Cummings, and Callie McGraw. Thanks for taking my call."

"It's not a good day, Eric. We just lost Lewis Amboy, a lineman supervisor in the field."

"Oh no, that's terrible."

There was a measured silence.

"What do you need, Eric? I have a lot going on right now."

"Callie McGraw from Sentinel Creek is here and wants us to start our Twin-Pac black-start unit to bring up the Franklin 500 kV line in order to get startup power to Torlon Hills. We need some kind of guidance from T&D to do this."

"How did she know the Franklin 500 kV line was repaired?" His voice sounded surprised.

Callie jumped in.

"Shane, I have been in close contact with Dale Morrison at Torlon. They are flirting with loss of decay heat removal and desperately require station service. He told me the line was ready."

"Callie, he is correct. However, the Twin-Pac cannot bring that 500 kV transformer and line back up. It will take one of the large GTs at Franklin. How quickly can you get one in service?"

Eric, Mike, and Teddy all looked at each other with vindication on their faces. Teddy spoke first.

"We told her that already. Do we have T&D's permission to energize the Franklin 500 kV line when we get one of our large GTs back into service?"

"Absolutely. Just coordinate it with SOC. I am aware that they need that line at Torlon Hills."

"Shane," Callie raised her voice, "I don't think Dale… Torlon Hills… has time for us to get one of the big GTs running. We can do this with the Twin-Pac."

"Callie, that 45 MVA generator on the Twin-Pac could not possibly energize the Franklin 500 kV transformer and bring that line up."

"Shane, the Twin-Pac is a 52.5 MVA generator built in the early sixties. It can do it."

There was a brief pause. Shane had to think.

"Callie, when you hit that dead 500 kV transformer with inrush current, I would be afraid it would shear the shaft or something on that generator. I would never risk it."

"The Twin-Pac can and will do it. It would be sitting with no load at 3600 RPM. It is two jet engines aerodynamically coupled with the generator. There is no hard coupling between the jet engines and the generator. The only inertia on the generator rotor is the two small, two-stage power turbines coupled to speed reducer into the generator. The jet engines are spinning freely. I would be more concerned about closing one of the big GTs running at synchronous speed than I would the Twin-Pac. It can take the hit, I am certain of it."

Again, there was a lengthy pause.

"Callie, Teddy, you two need to work this out. However you choose to do this works with me, but I would never attempt to use the Twin-Pac if I had a choice."

"We will take care of this," Teddy replied sanctimoniously. "I have to agree with you, Shane. I don't think it can be done. We need to bring up one of the main gas turbines."

They hung up the phone with Shane. Callie knew she must do something.

"Fine. Right now, can we just agree to get the Twin-Pac running? If we can't get it going, everything else is a moot point."

Eric, Mike, and Teddy looked at each other dismissively and then at Callie. Teddy answered first.

"That works. Let's see if we can get the Twin-Pac started." He then shook his head and defensively stated, "This may be problematic as cold as it is."

Mike Cummings paged Liz Anderson, the outside operator, to meet them at the Twin-Pac with the startup procedure. Liz was young, new, and inexperienced. Callie knew that if this was going to happen, it would be Mike Cummings and her making it happen.

After reviewing the startup procedure, Liz hesitantly selected START for the large two-cycle diesel truck engine that was used to spin up the gas turbine. It cranked slowly and labored. Aging lead-acid batteries abhor the cold. Liz cranked until the batteries lost enough voltage that the engine would barely turn.

Teddy looked almost relieved. He then looked at Eric while shaking his head.

"We must remove the batteries, take them to the maintenance shop, and charge them."

Callie was incensed.

"Just grab some jumper cables and we can jump it from the pickups!"

Teddy condescendingly stated, "Callie, it is a 24-volt system. The pickups are 12-volt. That won't work."

Callie was trying to keep her patience.

"We just need two sets of jumper cables, and we can connect the pickup batteries in series, not parallel. That doubles the voltage."

Teddy gave Eric a look like Callie was crazy.

"Eric?"

"She's right. If we connect the two pickup batteries in series, it will be 24 volts."

They removed the battery cables from the pickups to prevent damaging the pickup electrical systems and connected the batteries in series. Liz tried cranking again. This time it was much stronger. The engine was pushing lazy gray smoke out its exhaust but was not starting.

"Ether!" Callie said quickly. "We need some ether starting fluid!"

They found a can of ether starting fluid inside the enclosure. Eric told Liz to give it a little squirt. The engine knocked a few times, tried hard, but just could not quite get there.

Callie grabbed the ether starting fluid from Liz's hand and climbed partially up on the intake structure.

“My dad was a trucker for many years. I’ve watched him start these truck engines in the cold. Liz, as soon as I start spraying, you start cranking!”

Eric spun around on his heels toward Callie.

“You need to be careful with that stuff. You will blow a head gasket or worse!”

Callie nodded in partial agreement.

“We are running out of options. Just try and start it!”

Liz started cranking and Callie sprayed a continuous, steady stream of the starting fluid. The engine began perking up, and then made a series of deep, visceral rattles as the starting fluid detonated loudly in the cylinders. The engine then roared to life.

“Let it warm for a couple of minutes, Liz!” Callie hollered over the high-pitched noise of the two-cycle diesel engine.

Eric looked miffed but did not say anything.

After they gave the engine a few minutes to warm, Callie looked at Liz.

“Engage the torque converter and start spinning the turbine up to light-off RPM.”

The diesel RPM increased steadily as the Twin-Pac began spooling up in speed. At light-off speed, she watched the fuel valves sequence. It lit.

The speed increased.

The noise of the Twin-Pac became deafening, especially with several of the access doors open. Eric and Teddy stepped back with their eyes wide. Callie remained focused on the vibration and exhaust temperature. Both were hovering between yellow and red.

The generator made it to 3600 RPM and Callie parked it there. The vibration and temperature calmed, and the Twin-Pac’s heart was beating loud and strong.

They left Liz at the Twin-Pac and rushed back to the control room. The switching operations had to be done from the consoles.

Back in the control room, she gathered Teddy, Eric, and Mike and addressed them sternly.

"The Twin-Pac is running. We don't have time to prepare and spin up one of the unit gas turbines. It has to be the Twin-Pac that energizes the Franklin 500 kV line."

Teddy looked at Callie sternly and said, "I don't agree or approve of this. It is on you when this fails!"

It was awkward, but Callie didn't waver. She had been pushed into these corners many times in her career. She knew what she must do.

"Since Teddy has made it perfectly clear this is on me, I am making the decision to energize the Franklin 500 kV transformer and Franklin line to Torlon Hills."

She then waved Alex Cordon over to her.

"Alex, I need you to temporarily disable the underfrequency relays for the yard and the Twin-Pac. It is the only way this will get done."

Alex puttered around for a few minutes but had no idea how to disable the relays. Callie lost patience and showed him.

It was time to energize the switchyard. This part was easy. It was called a dead-bus closure. There was nothing to synchronize. Callie turned to Eric.

"We must call the SOC and tell them we are energizing the Franklin 500 kV bus in your switchyard. I would let them know the transformer is next, and then the line."

Eric called the, now, primary SOC in Ohio and reached the current SOC supervisor.

"This is Franklin Generating Station and we are about to energize our 500 kV bus using the Twin-Pac black-start generator. When the bus is energized, we will attempt to power up the 500 kV transformer to Torlon Hills."

The SOC supervisor was surprised and caught a little off guard.

"You can do this with the Twin-Pac?" he asked incredulously.

"Callie McGraw is here, and she thinks we can do this."

"You have our permission to try." He paused. "I hope you have a Plan B if that doesn't work because I know the situation at Torlon Hills is not good right now. They need power."

They hung up the phone. Callie looked at Eric. The phone rang once on the console. Eric handed it to her without looking away from the mimic. Dale's voice came through the speaker, strained and breathless.

"Callie… Train A is knocking hard now. Herman says we may have minutes."

Callie took a breath.

"Close the breaker and energize the 500 kV bus."

When the Twin-Pac generator breaker closed, the Franklin switchyard came to life. The Twin-Pac never flinched.

“Dale, we just energized the Franklin 500 kV bus. We are doing the 500 kV transformer next. We will call you right back.”

They hung up the phone. Eric hovered over the one-line mimic on the display, eyes moving between the energized 500 kV bus and the dead gray beyond it. The next step was the first of several difficult ones. She had to energize the huge 500 kV transformer.

“You’re really going to close the Twin-Pac into a 500 kV step-up transformer?” Eric asked incredulously.

“I’m going to close into dead iron,” Callie said. “And then we’re going to see whether the Twin-Pac generator is as healthy as the attested paperwork claims it is.”

She looked directly into Teddy’s eyes. He looked away.

Mike glanced at the settings screen. “What if we go underfrequency?”

"It won't trip with the underfrequency relay disabled," Callie replied. "We're giving the governor time to catch the dip. Three to five seconds at the most. Then we enable the frequency relay."

She didn't raise her voice. She didn't need to. The room already had the kind of quiet that came when people understood the outcome wouldn't be negotiated.

Callie picked up the phone again and got Dale on the second ring.

"Tell me you've got something," he said. "We are going to lose Train A anytime. It is knocking loudly now."

"We have the Twin-Pac running. It appears to be stable. In this cold it should be able to hold forty megawatts, and it knows it."

"That's enough," Dale said. He sounded like a man holding a door shut with his shoulder. "Herman says B-train diesel is still not ready and A-train is on its way out."

Callie didn't waste any time.

"Here's the path," she said. "We're going to energize the 500 kV transformer, then the Franklin 500 kV line segment, then your station service transformer. Nothing else. No feeders. No 'helpful' closes. You keep the Torlon station service transformer dead until I tell you to close it in."

Dale exhaled once. "What do you need?"

"I need Herman to treat this like a dead-bus receipt. They don't close anything until we tell them. No auto transfers. No load pickup. Just the essential bus, controlled."

"I'll get it done," Dale said.

Callie ended the call and turned back to Eric and Mike.

"This is the physics," she said, tapping the mimic lightly. "When we energize big iron, we're not picking up homes. We're feeding magnetizing current. It's a reactive hit. The Twin-Pac will feel it like a gut punch. It will sag. It will groan. And if the exciter is tired, or the AVR is lazy, it'll fall over."

Eric stared at the breaker icon.

"One shot," he said.

"Not one," Callie answered. "But not many."

She pointed to the sequence she had already written on a notepad. It was simple enough that nobody could pretend to misunderstand it later.

Step one: Confirm Twin-Pac stable. Frequency steady. Voltage steady. Field current not wandering. No alarms trending. They were there now.

Step two: Confirm Franklin station-service bus isolated. Every nonessential breaker open. If you accidentally pick up a regional feeder, you lose the machine.

Step three: Pre-stage relay coordination. Bypass the underfrequency relay long enough to survive the first dip, not so long to destroy itself.

Step four: Close into the step-up transformer only. No line. No remote bus. Just iron.

Step five: Let the machine recover. If it does not recover cleanly, we open and we stop.

Step six: Energize the transmission segment toward Torlon, the shortest practical path. Watch voltage like it's a pulse.

Step seven: When Torlon confirms dead-bus ready, close into the station service transformer and bring it up. Then it is only a matter of synchronizing the essential bus to the frequency of the Twin-Pac and the Franklin 500 kV line.

Eric swallowed. "Okay."

Callie didn't soften it.

"We do it in that order because it gives us failure points we can still walk away from. Once you energize the long line and then lose the Twin-Pac, you don't 'try again.' You inherit a half-alive system you can't control."

Mike nodded, then asked the right question.

"What about line charging? We're going to see voltage run away if it's too light."

"We keep the segment short," Callie said. "We don't energize the world. And we accept that the AVR is going to be busy. The longer the line, the more charging vars it demands. If we only energize the Torlon segment, the Twin-Pac might hold the voltage long enough to get their station service transformer alive."

She leaned closer, voice flat.

"If voltage climbs out of range, we open. If frequency collapses and keeps falling, we open. We are not going to grind this generator into dust trying to be heroes."

Eric's finger hovered over the first breaker control.

Callie watched the frequency indicator. Sixty, steady. She watched the field current. Calm. The Twin-Pac was as ready as it would ever be.

Eric hesitated. "What about the line relays?"

"If the distance relays see something they interpret as a fault and trip, we're done," Callie said. "But telemetry to the yard is unreliable and we don't have ten extra minutes. We try it as-is."

"Close the step-up," she said.

The Twin-Pac groaned and the fuel valves poured fuel into the combustion chambers. There was a surge of black smoke out of the Twin-Pac stacks.

Frequency sagged immediately to 58.2, then didn't glide back. It lunged. The governor overfed, caught itself, then overcorrected again before settling into something that resembled sixty hertz. The old mechanical governor didn't think. It reacted. And it reacted late.

The exhaust tone dropped, deeper, heavier, the Twin-Pac's two jet engines audibly taking fuel as the governor tried to hold speed. A vibration moved through the floor and into the console.

Field current spiked hard. Voltage dipped and then surged as the automatic voltage regulator shoved to keep it alive. Alarms chirped once, then quieted as the machine clawed itself back into shape.

Callie didn't move. She didn't blink. She waited until the trend lines flattened again.

"Good," she said. "The exciter's definitely awake."

Eric exhaled like he'd been holding his breath for a year.

"We're holding."

"Yes," Callie replied. "So far, so good."

She stared at the next breaker. It energized the 500 kV line segment toward Torlon.

"Same rule," she said. "If it starts to pull us down, we open. No debate."

Eric looked at her. "Ready?"

Callie took a breath.

"Now."

The line breaker closed. The Twin-Pac dug in. Frequency dipped again, 58.6, then fought back as fuel opened and the engines dug in harder. Voltage rose slightly with the line's charging effect. The AVR pushed it back down into range like a hand pressing a lid onto boiling water.

Callie watched the numbers and spoke in the same voice she used when she taught people how to recover a black plant.

"We have a path."

Eric stared at the energized segment like it was a miracle. Callie didn't let him admire it. This process was far from over.

"I'm calling Dale."

He answered almost immediately.

"Callie, please tell me you have power to give us." He reached out and grabbed Herman Distel by the arm. "It's Callie at Franklin," he said in the background.

Herman took the phone from him.

"This is Herman."

"We have an energized path to your yard," Callie said with no drama in her voice. "500 kV line segment is hot. We're stable at sixty hertz. Voltage is good."

Herman looked at the essential-bus mimic at Torlon breaker control.

"What do you need?"

"I need you to close in your station service transformer with low-side breakers open. Once it is energized, you will have to synchronize your essential-service bus to it."

Herman turned to the board operator.

"Verify our station service transformer is open on all low-side feeds."

The operator read back each breaker position carefully. No guessing. No assumptions.

"All open. Bus dead. No residual voltage."

Herman went back to the phone.

"We are dead and ready."

"Good," Callie said. "Close the breaker into your station service transformer."

As soon as the station service transformer at Torlon closed, the Twin-Pac hiccuped, the frequency bounced, but recovered much more quickly this time. It was a substantially smaller transformer than the 500 kV unit on the Franklin line.

Herman smiled at Dale and the other operators standing there.

"Callie, we have our station service transformer energized."

"We're stable. Synchronize your essential bus."

"We are synchronized and ready to close," Herman replied.

"Do it. Then unload Train A slowly. The Twin-Pac will pick up the load as the frequency drops."

"Roger that. We will synchronize to the essential-services bus and unload Train A." He repeated it clearly.

Callie watched as the load increased on the Twin-Pac.

5 MW.

7 MW.

12 MW.

The Twin-Pac leaned into the added load, but it did not sag dangerously this time. The reactive insult had already been absorbed. This was real power now, measurable and steady.

15 MW.

24 MW.

31 MW.

Steady. Holding.

“Callie.”

“We’re holding on our end,” she said before he asked.

Herman exhaled. The men around him all clapped their hands and cheered.

“Callie, we have unloaded Train A and shut it down. You are carrying us now.”

“That’s all we need,” she replied. “We will monitor the Twin-Pac closely and let you know if it starts complaining.”

Herman looked at the essential bus again. It was alive. He spoke carefully.

"You just bought us time."

There was a pause on the other end.

"Then use it well," Callie said. "Get your other diesel train operational as soon as possible. You are depending on a sixty-year-old gas turbine unit that is showing its age in every arena."

Callie didn't celebrate. She watched the frequency trace for another full minute. Machines that old had a habit of failing just when you began trusting them.

Outside Torlon, transmission towers still lay twisted in rights-of-way. The grid was still black across hundreds of miles. But inside one nuclear station, one essential bus hummed. Not triumph. Not recovery. Just time.

And for the first time since the collapse, time was something they controlled.

***

Field Operations / Eastern Region

Dave Carter called Shane and Garrin. He was still partially in shock.

"The helicopter just lifted Lewis out. They're taking his body to the hospital."

***

Part 14

Reality Lands

****

The MidAtlantic Grid

The storm moved offshore during the following night. It did not weaken. It reorganized. The pressure gradient tightened behind it, and the wind shifted northwest. Temperatures fell into single digits. What had been glaze became armor. What had sagged now froze in place. Ice does not release when the sky clears. It hardens.

Across the eastern corridors, transmission lines hung lower than design. Conductors no longer hummed; they creaked. In the early light, the lattice structures wore thick sleeves of frozen weight that glittered in a sun offering no heat. Access roads that had been slush the day before were now polished concrete. Bucket truck crews could not climb what they could not reach.

Line crews stood at the edge of rights-of-way and did math in their heads. One tower down was manageable. Five was a mobilization. Ten was a campaign.

Helicopters lifted when visibility allowed. From above, the damage was geometric and indifferent. Steel folded at calculated angles. Crossarms twisted. Insulator strings snapped and lay in arcs across frozen ground. No smoke. No flame. Just structure that no longer existed. Restoration was no longer about switching. It was about cranes.

Helicopter crews stopped looking for damage and instead simply categorized it. Bent members meant reinforcement. Broken crossarms meant replacement. A tower folded at mid-span meant cranes, steel, and time. It was a mathematical calculation, the least work for the highest return.

They coordinated with the linemen on the ground who were also doing triage to develop a sensible plan and approach to restoration.

***

The Cities

In the cities and towns throughout the service area, the second day felt different. The first night had been inconvenient. Blankets. Flashlights. Candles. Families gathered in living rooms as if camping indoors. Two days into the outage, inconvenience had hardened into arithmetic. Children no longer treated their breath as a novelty. The novelty had worn thin.

Grocery stores without power became open air warehouses with dwindling food supplies. Refrigerators failed requiring extreme diligence from store managers. If the store still had heat, the refrigerated food thawed. If the store lost all heat, the refrigerated food remained safe, while everything else froze. Much of it being damaged by the freeze. Cans swelled, bottled liquids broke from the expanding ice within.

Managers stood in aisles doing quiet arithmetic. What could be saved. What would have to be thrown away.

People came to the hard reality that refrigeration is invisible until it stops. Then, everyone notices.

Plumbing became a crucible of silent, far-reaching impairment. Pipes froze and the results weren't known until they thawed and their contents destroyed sheetrock, floors, and electrical.

Cell service remained spotty to non-existent as tower batteries drained. Some sites had generators. Many did not. Text messages went through. Calls did not.

Hospitals were still running. For now. Medical workers that were at work during the event now found themselves anchored there due to demand, attrition, and spotty to non-existent replacement workers. Their emergency departments operated under generator power, every nonessential circuit dark. Diesel fuel inventories were counted in minutes and hours, not days and weeks. Fuel delivery routes were theoretical.

Blood and plasma supplies ran thin. Accident rates in homes and businesses increased dramatically. Minor broken bones were no longer considered high priorities in triage. Concussions, and blood loss victims were moved to the top of the list. A staple of severe ice storms was concussions, the injuries from falls were continuous. The elderly dominated the epidemic.

Carbon monoxide incidents began appearing as residents attempted to heat living spaces with gas appliances and portable generators.

Bandages and consumables were quietly rationed as the trucks needed for replenishment were parked due to no drivers, no fuel, or no inventory to load.

Nursing and assisted living facilities were hit the hardest overall. The elderly, infirm, and handicapped were subject to extreme cold and lack of care from nursing personnel who, themselves, were struggling with their own families and home drama.

Those who remained in the care facilities were tasked with making the calls to loved ones that no one wanted to receive.

Police departments moved officers into the most trouble-prone intersections where signals remained black. Accidents were slower now, less violent, more frequent. Ice does not allow speed, but it does not forgive mistakes.

***

MARES - SOC

At MARES, the wall was still mostly gray, though color had begun to return in small patches, thanks entirely to the interties with the four neighboring independent system operators.

The Northern Area Independent System Operator (NAISO), Western Area Independent System Operator (WAISO), Southern Electric Independent System Operator (SEISO), and Lower Atlantic Independent System Operator (LAISO), were able to provide small, meaningful power flows to regional feeders off the interties.

Far more important than this, all the other regions were loaning linemen, components, and construction crews.

Without them, it would be months, not days or weeks in the rebuild.

Small islands now existed. Western pockets held. Redstone Valley was back on station service. Torlon Hills was alive by wire and faith, still requiring permanent station service and not the possibly fickle Twin-Pac. East of the Harbor substation, entire corridors were still silent. The triage teams shuddered as they pushed east in their efforts. The closer to the coast they went, the damage increased in numbers and scope.

Operators in the secondary SOC no longer spoke in megawatts. They spoke in materials. Poles. Insulators. Transformers. Lead times. This was no longer an electrical event. It was a structural one.

***

Langford – Harrisburg

The western headquarters of MidAtlantic sat just outside Harrisburg, a low glass-and-steel structure built for proximity to transmission corridors rather than prestige.

Inside, the lights were on… Selectively. Half the building remained dark to conserve load. The executive floor operated on a diesel back-up generator. Elevators cycled intermittently. HVAC ran in short, disciplined intervals.

On the MARES wall display in Stephen Langford's office, the MARES map remained largely gray east of Harbor. Thin threads of color crept inward from the interties. They were conditional, and still fragile.

Kendall Allen stepped cautiously to the executive suite and asked to see Stephen Langford. Leah led him into Stephen's office.

Stephen looked up when they entered his office.

"Kendall?"

Kendall lowered his head slightly and spoke evenly.

"Stephen, we just lost a man, a MidAtlantic lineman, who was doing triage on the grid. His name was Lewis Amboy. He has family here in this area."

Stephen pursed his lips, and squinted slightly.

“Hmmm. I understand that can be a very dangerous job. Has the legal department and HR been notified? These things can get out of control very quickly.”

Kendall was perplexed, even astonished. He expected a very different reaction.

“Yes. Both.” He said slowly.

“Good. Let them do their jobs.”

He stared at Kendall another moment.

“Did you have anything else?”

“No, that’s all. I just thought you would like to know.”

“Thanks, Kendall.”

Kendall left Stephen’s office shaken by the exchange.

Beyond the windows, the Susquehanna moved beneath a skin of broken ice.

Kendall walked slowly down the hall to his office. It seemed to be a different place than it had a few hours prior. He sat down and rested his head in his hands, contemplating.

Approximately an hour or so later Leah stepped quietly back into Stephen's office.

"Senator Halcott on line one."

Stephen lifted the receiver.

"Bill? It's been a while. What can I do for you?"

"Stephen. I assume you understand the political gravity of what we're dealing with?" The Senator's voice was measured, calm, practiced.

"I do," Stephen replied. "The eastern transmission corridors suffered structural failures. Reconstruction is underway. Crews are mobilizing across…"

The Senator interrupted.

"I'm not calling for a field report. The capital region is still largely dark. Federal facilities are on generator power. Stephen, that is not sustainable." He paused and took a deep breath. "You could even call it a national security emergency."

Stephen glanced at the map again.

"Harbor Substation depends on multiple transmission paths," he said evenly. "Several of those structures are down. Restoration is sequential. It is not discretionary."

"Sequence doesn't help me" the senator replied. "I'm interested in stability. My colleagues are already asking why redundancy failed. Why winterization was insufficient. Why a grid of this scale collapsed."

There it was. Not outright accusation. It was initial positioning. Stephen knew it was coming, as certain as the sun rises. He had lived it in other economies over and over.

"We are prioritizing nuclear station service restoration," Stephen said. "Decay heat removal is non-negotiable."

"I understand the nuclear issues," the senator said. "My constituents only understand cold apartments, frozen pipes, and no food. The press is already assembling an on-going death toll, and it is looking very bad."

A pause.

"What I need," the senator continued, "is a timeline I can defend publicly. Seventy-two hours. Ninety-six. Something credible. Give me something to go on."

Stephen studied the damage matrix on the laptop sitting beside him. Towers. Insulators. Access constraints. Crane mobilization schedules. Weather windows.

"There is no credible seventy-two-hour full restoration," he said.

"Then give me a partial one," the senator replied. "Harbor. Federal district. Major hospitals. Some kind of time frame for visible progress."

Visible. That word hung like laundry on a clothesline. Stephen's mind calculated the damage differently, not in steel or conductors, but in political fallout and stock implications. He knew action was essential and critical.

"I will review resource allocation," Stephen said carefully.

"Please do," the senator replied. "Because hearings are inevitable. It would be better if they occur during recovery rather than failure."

The line went quiet. Stephen lowered the receiver slowly. Outside, the river ice shifted with a muted crack. He pressed a button on his desk.

"Leah, did Fred Samson make it in today?"

Fred Samson was the MidAtlantic Corporate Communication Director. Stephen had worked with him at two previous companies and brought him to MidAtlantic not long after he took over.

Fred entered Stephen's office with a smile on his face. As always, he was impeccably groomed in a fresh suit. Appearances were everything to him.

"Stephen, so good to see you! I am relatively certain I know why I am here."

Stephen stood and shook his hand.

“That’s why I brought you with me to MidAtlantic Energy. I need someone who remains on top of things. You are a model of that person.”

“Thank you, Stephen.”

Stephen sat down and put his hands behind his head, leaning back in his chair.

“We are in the middle of a reputational nightmare. People will quickly forget the problem was the weather. They will try and blame the power company. I need your strongest performance ever on this one, Fred. Bring your A-game to the table.”

“You have my word, Stephen.” He grinned broadly. “You know this won’t be cheap, right?”

“Spend the money, Fred. Perception is 99% of the game. You know that more than anyone I have ever met. We need to be seen as the ones who helped our customers through this weather nightmare that no one foresaw”.

Fred nodded his head vigorously.

"Multiple statements will be drafted with emphasis on resilience, emphasis on unprecedented severity, and emphasis on inter-regional cooperation. We will control the overall optics and ensure they align with the truth that MidAtlantic is going out of our way to restore what was destroyed by this unprecedented weather event."

"Fred, you are a master. Make it happen."

Stephen stood and shook his hand again. Fred left Stephen's office with a mandate and vigor.

Stephen was preparing to leave his office for the day when Leah stepped back in.

"There's another call you may want to take."

Stephen did not look up immediately.

"From whom?"

"Harry Halvorsen."

That made him pause. He remembered Harry. He was measured, technical, immune to flattery or charm. Stephen picked up the phone.

"Stephen Langford."

"Good morning, Stephen."

The voice was steady. Neither warm nor hostile.

"You may remember me."

"I do," Stephen said. "You elected to leave during restructuring."

A soft exhale on the other end. Not laughter.

"Yes," Harry said. "That is one way to describe it."

Silence followed. Not awkward, but intentional.

"Harry, this is not an ideal morning. What can I do for you?"

"It isn't what you can do for me," Harry replied. "It's what you're about to do for yourself."

Stephen leaned back slightly.

"I'm listening."

"I watched the grid fail," Harry said. "Not dramatically, but predictably."

Stephen did not respond. Harry continued.

"When capital allocation shifts from structural hardening to quarterly financial efficiency, resilience becomes optional. Optional systems eventually reveal themselves."

"You're calling to debate financial strategy?" Stephen asked tersely.

"No," Harry said. "I'm calling because I was just contacted by someone from the Senate Energy Committee."

That changed the air. Stephen didn't speak.

"I had sent them a large amount of information several months ago and never heard back. For some reason, they are now reaching out to me."

Harry exhaled with a faint smile.

"Apparently, they're now interested in assembling extensive background information on procurement decisions, deferred winterization capital, executive incentive structures, and certain vendor relationships."

"Vendor relationships?" Stephen asked.

"Yes," Harry said calmly. "Aegis Data Management, for example. A now prominent "smart" data management software company that supplies cost-optimized source to recycling material and parts control across several of your assets. A firm that you have a significant stake in, if I recall correctly."

Stephen's tone did not change.

"ADM was fully vetted, this is old news. What's your point?"

"It was vetted for legality, Stephen, not for prudence."

Another pause.

"You hired Calvin Johnson as the VP of nuclear shortly after that episode," Harry continued. "An attorney. Capable. Loyal. Certainly not a nuclear engineer."

"That appointment was fully within my authority."

"Of course it was," Harry said. "Just as reallocating winterization reserves was within your authority. Just as reducing structural redundancy was within your authority."

There was no accusation in his voice. Only sequencing.

"You're suggesting causation," Stephen said emphatically.

"I'm suggesting alignment," Harry replied. "Incentives shape outcomes. Outcomes eventually surface."

The river ice shifted outside with a dull fracture.

"What do you want, Harry?"

"Nothing," he said. "I'm well beyond wanting."

Silence again.

"I kept my documentation," Harry continued. "Board minutes. Capital reclassification memos. Internal risk analysis labeled "improbable."

Stephen's expression did not change.

"I am relatively certain the Committee will ask whether the collapse was weather," Harry said, "or whether it was governance."

"And just what will you tell them, Harry?"

"The truth," Harry replied. "That the system performed exactly as incentivized."

That landed harder than any accusation could have.

"Are you implying negligence."

"I'm implying entropy," Harry said. "Engineers design margins. Executives trim them. Politicians defend the trimming. Eventually physics votes just as it did in this storm." He paused. "Physics always wins, Stephen, and politicians always shift."

Stephen's voice remained controlled.

"Harry, if you truly believe there was wrongdoing, maybe you should hire counsel and pursue it formally." Stephen was uncharacteristically agitated.

"There was no wrongdoing," Harry said quietly. "That's the point. Everything was permissible."

Another pause.

"Maybe someday you will come to terms with the simple, immutable fact that permissible and prudent are not synonyms."

Stephen did not answer.

"I'm not calling to threaten you," Harry continued. "I'm calling because you're about to enter hearings, and you'll be tempted to describe this as unforeseeable."

"And it wasn't?"

"It was unlikely," Harry said. "Which is different."

Silence stretched between them.

"Don't you think you're being overly dramatic?" Stephen said at last.

"No," Harry replied. "I was always cautious, careful, and took the high road. You know this. You looked deep into my files and the job I did when I was at MidAtlantic. I was not a troublemaker. I faithfully kept MidAtlantic out of trouble. In fact, it was my job before you eliminated the position."

Another terse silence.

"Good luck, Stephen. I am relatively certain you will need it."

The line went dead.

Stephen held the receiver a moment longer before setting it down. He stared at the mostly gray MARES map, compiling actions in his mind. ADM had reduced costs. Hiring Calvin Johnson reduced friction and added a legal resource to a volatile nuclear system. Winterization reserves had improved margins. Each decision was defensible; each decision was rational.

Outside, the ice shifted again. He pressed the intercom.

“Leah.”

“Yes?”

“From now on, I will take all calls from Mr. Halvorsen.”

***

MARES SOC

Samuel Tribetti was back on the floor before the coffee finished dripping. The dimly glowing mimic wall was no longer a catastrophe. It was a puzzle. Color had returned in narrow corridors. Small victories. Few of them were decisive but progress was being made.

His phone rang.

"This is Dale Morrison at Torlon Hills, do you have a moment?"

Samuel didn't look up from the grid topology map he was studying.

"You've got something for me?"

"We do," Dale said. "Torlon Hills Diesel train B is operational. We've got a backup again."

Samuel exhaled slowly. That mattered. It took some pressure off him.

"And Train A?"

"Glycol contaminated oil. The bearings are damaged. It is down for the foreseeable future.

A brief silence.

"Then why are you calling?" Samuel asked.

"Because we can now free-up Franklin Generating Station for load use."

That got his attention.

"Explain."

"The Twin-Pac carried us through the night," Dale said. "But it's maxed. If we reload our diesel Train B and back the Twin-Pac down, Franklin can bring up GT-1. Once that's stable, we can transition completely off the Twin-Pac."

Samuel's eyes moved across the eastern side of the map.

"And?"

"And we can use the Cornell 230 kV completion. Blackstone can come up on startup power from Sentinel Creek. Once Blackstone is synchronized, we push through Dixie and energize the Canvoy lateral. That gives you a live path into Harbor from the south."

Samuel did not answer immediately.

He traced the path mentally.

Sentinel → Dominion → Spearville → Willow → Condor → Cornell → Blackstone → Dixie → Southpoint → Canvoy → Harbor. It was tight. But it could work.

"You're assuming Franklin GT-1 holds," Samuel said.

"We won't move until it does."

"And frequency?"

"We unload the Twin-Pac slowly. Bring Train B up to carry our essential bus. We can raise line frequency slightly using a controlled margin. This will give Franklin breathing room. Then light Franklin's GT-1."

Samuel considered it. The eastern seaboard sat dark on his wall. Harbor was political. Torlon was existential. Blackstone was leverage.

"Has Kendall signed off?" he asked.

Dale hesitated.

"I haven't discussed it with him yet. I was hoping we could keep it at our level."

Samuel allowed himself the smallest smile.

"She's driving this, isn't she?"

Dale paused to consider the consequences.

"Yes."

"Have Callie call me."

***

Franklin

Between catnaps in the Franklin lunch room, Callie had been studying all the line status updates constantly being posted from MARES. She had the grid topology map firmly embedded in her mind. She could visualize every possible energization arrangement like a chess master anticipates a move. She had discussed several options with Dale already. She knew Dale was going to call Samuel Tribetti when his diesel was available.

The anticipated call arrived several minutes later.

"Callie, you are on speaker with Samuel Tribetti. I have told him what you think should be done."

"Hi, Samuel."

"Callie, I think your plan is as good as any I have seen for energizing back to Harbor. It gets the monkey off everyone's back and if it works, solidifies Dale's backup power at Torlon. I went ahead and called Kendall Allen and his group. They hemmed and hawed a bit, but they signed off on it." He paused before carefully continuing. "I left you out of the conversation with Kendall."

"That was prudent." Callie said quietly. She then gave an audible sigh of relief and stated, "I think it is the best path forward. As soon as Dale has his diesel issue corrected, we can execute."

Dale jumped in.

"Callie, We're ready here at Torlon. Train – B diesel is fully operational. You can call the shots at Franklin."

Callie nodded her head.

"Roger that. We will move forward now."

Callie stood at the control console with Teddy, Eric, and Mike.

The Twin-Pac was steady but tired. Old machines have a tone when they'd given enough. The Twin-Pac took on that tone many years earlier.

Callie's phone lit up. It was Dale again. She put it on speaker mode.

"Train B is ready," Dale's voice called out loudly.

"Synchronize it to the essential bus," Callie said. "We'll start unloading the Twin-Pac five megawatts at a time. Let us know if the diesel is not keeping up."

A few minutes later the load on the Twin-Pac began to shift.

Thirty-one megawatts became twenty-six.

Twenty-six became twenty-two.

The Twin-Pac's exhaust note lightened.

At Torlon, diesel Train B took the weight.

Frequency steadied.

"Bring Train B up another five," Callie said. "We want margin before we move."

When the Twin-Pac settled below fifteen megawatts, she nodded.

"Franklin now has room to start equipment, including the surge amps."

Eric looked at her.

"You're serious."

"Yes."

She adjusted the governor reference slightly. Frequency crept upward within allowable tolerance. Not dramatic. Just enough to create space.

"Line-up your GT-1," she said confidently.

Mike Cummings went with Liz out into the frigid plant to align, fill, and prepare the system for operation. Callie watched the Twin-Pac intently. If the diesel went down at Torlon, the Twin-Pac governor would immediately try and grab that load. Depending on how quick it happened, it may not succeed. A shudder ran down her back.

After several minutes staring at the displays, she became cognizant of just how exhausted she was. She sat for a moment and dozed, oblivious of the activity picking up in the control room as they prepared to fire GT – 1. The next thing she remembered was Don Garcia gently nudging her.

"Do you want to watch GT – 1 roll and fire?"

She was disheveled for a few moments. Her neck was stiff. She shook it off.

"Thanks for waking me. Yes, yes I do."

Outside, the big turbine spun up to 800 RPM for the mandatory purge cycle to ensure no combustibles were present in the HRSG equipment. The 12 minutes seemed long to her. Her little unit was only 9 minutes. The purge ended, the turbine dropped to 500 RPM and lit. The distinctive, guttural rumble of combustion resonance was felt throughout the plant immediately after light-off. She always found this exhilarating.

Callie watched the speed climb. As the speed increased, the combustion resonance eased off.

When GT-1 synchronized, the board changed color. There was now real generation. Not borrowed time.

“Transfer your auxiliaries,” Callie said quietly to Don.

She called Dale.

“You can take your diesel offline and into standby operation. Franklin is stable on GT – 1. We really need some load on this machine because we are out of emission compliance. Start bringing up your normal auxiliaries. It will help our stability here.”

Over the next hour Franklin’s GT – 1 would pick up load in multiple sized blocks as the Torlon Hills plant brought all their non-critical auxiliaries back to life. When this leveled out, her phone rang. It was Dale.

“Am I on speaker?” He asked hesitantly.

“No. I am in the lunchroom. Alone.”

He lowered his voice slightly anyway.

"Callie, you are amazing. I don't have a clue what would have happened had you not been there."

She smiled warmly, and quietly said, "Don't get sentimental on me. We still have a long way to go. I am leaving in a bit for Millstone Junction to check on my folks, and then heading back to Sentinel Creek. "

"Callie, thanks again."

"You owe me Mr. Morrison. Someday. Steak and Seafood again."

"You can bank on it, Ms. McGraw. Drive carefully."

Millstone Junction

Callie napped for a few hours in a chair in the lunchroom at Franklin. She was exhausted. Her back hurt. She was filthy from crawling around on the Twin-Pac. However, she knew she must get to Millstone Junction to see her parents before returning to Sentinel Creek.

The trip was slow. Cars were still off the road facing every point in the compass as if they were toys arranged by a toddler. Many were badly damaged. The press was having a heyday with this.

The turn into Millstone Junction felt smaller than she remembered. Ice still glazed the shoulders of the road, though the main lane had been sanded into a dull gray ribbon. The town's old sugar maples lined the street like veterans who had stood too long in bad weather. Some no longer stood at all.

Branches lay scattered across lawns, thick as fence rails. One red oak in front of the Methodist church was split cleanly down to the trunk, its interior pale and exposed like bone. The eastern white pines fared worse. Their crowns, once soft and feathery against the sky, now hung torn and lopsided, entire tops snapped under the weight. Ice does not negotiate with age.

Callie slowed as she turned into her parents' gravel drive. The old maple at the corner of the yard, the one she started climbing when she was seven or eight, had lost half its canopy. The remaining limbs reached unevenly toward a sky that had already forgotten the storm.

She sat in the car for a moment longer than necessary. The house was dark except for a faint orange flickering in the front window. It was the fireplace.

She stepped out. The air had the brittle feel of single digits. Snow crunched hard beneath her boots. When she opened the front door, the cold inside met her halfway. The living room smelled of wood smoke and damp wool. Her mother rose slowly from the couch wrapped in two heavy blankets, her father from the recliner near the hearth.

"Callie?"

No theatrics. Just relief.

She crossed the room in three steps and wrapped her arms around both of them at once. They were thinner than she remembered. Or maybe just colder. Emotion overwhelmed her for a moment. A few pent-up tears rolled down her cheeks.

"You shouldn't have come," her father said quietly.

“I was passing through. I have to get back to Sentinel Creek as soon as possible.”

Her mother pulled back and studied her face.

“You look horrible!”

“Thanks Mom. I am fine.”

The fire snapped behind them. The rest of the house lay in shadows.

“The piping?” Callie asked.

“Kitchen’s frozen,” her father said. “Bathroom’s close. We’re letting the faucets drip where we can.”

She nodded automatically, already calculating. She glanced toward the front window.

“The maple,” she said softly.

Her father followed her gaze.

“Lost the south side,” he said. “Forty years of growth in about six hours.”

Neither of them said anything for a moment. The room held that peculiar quiet of a house without electricity. There was no hum, no refrigerator compressor noise, no distant television murmur. Just frozen breath, a gently crackling fire, and wood shifting.

Her mother touched her sleeve.

“We’re fine honey.”

Callie swallowed.

“I know.”

She did not tell them about the diesel at Torlon, or the transformer, or the Twin-Pac hunting at fifty-eight hertz. She just stood there long enough for the warmth of the fire to soak through her coat.

“I can’t stay,” she said.

Her father nodded once. He always understood duty in others even when he disliked it.

“You get the lights back on,” he said. “It’s what you do.”

She leaned down and kissed her mother’s forehead, then her father’s. When she stepped back outside, the sky was clear and hard and indifferent. The broken limbs of the maple creaked faintly as the temperature dropped another degree.

She paused beside the car and ran her hand over the rough bark of what remained. Old growth takes decades to build. One night to break. She got in the car and drove back toward Sentinel Creek, the town shrinking behind her, dark except for the one house she knew so well with a working fireplace.

***

Sentinel Creek

Callie arrived back at Sentinel, running on adrenaline only. She never had a chance to even sit down. She had previously instructed her operators to have Sentinel Creek's GT and steam turbine ready before she arrived. They were still running with the black start diesels only.

After a quick walk-through of the plant, she called Samuel Tribetti at SOC.

She asked anxiously, "Cornell line status?"

"It just cleared inspection about twenty minutes ago. They think it is ready to energize."

She turned to her control room operator.

"Let's close the switchyard breaker 2901 to energize Cornell 230 KV line."

The 230 kV segment came alive.

Blackstone's operators were already in position.

"Blackstone ready to receive startup power."

"Close in your auxiliary transformer," Callie said.

Another pause.

"We have auxiliaries."

That mattered. Combined cycle capacity meant stability. Sentinel then rolled their GT – 1 and synchronized to the available lines which included the Cornell 230 KV to Blackstone. She called and gave them the okay to proceed with start-up.

On the roll-up, Blackstone – 1 failed to light. It was an ongoing maintenance issue that was never correctly addressed. They had to pivot to GT – 2. Luckily, it lit and synchronized.

When Blackstone synchronized, the southern corridor strengthened.

"Proceed to Dixie," she said.

Voltage moved eastward. Segment by segment power was restored. It wasn't dramatic, but the victories were mounting.

At Harbor Substation, a breaker indicator shifted from gray to red. Then another. A distribution feeder came alive in the eastern districts. Police radios crackled with reports of traffic lights returning. Inside apartments, thermostats clicked, and this time heat followed.

Blackstone and Sentinel Creek began loading. Hard. Each feeder pulled heavy load as homes and businesses rushed to catch up.

Samuel watched the map. Small islands were beginning to touch. He picked up the phone.

“Notify Stephen Langford and the Senator’s office,” he said. “Harbor substation is receiving controlled power from the southern corridor.” He paused. “Emphasis on controlled.

***

Part 15

Pressure Without Noise

****

Color crept across the MARES wall in narrow, disciplined corridors. Harbor stabilized under controlled load. Blackstone carried more than it had been designed to carry during winter shoulder months. Sentinel ran hard but steady. Torlon's essential bus was no longer a question mark.

At Sentinel Creek, Callie did not feel triumphant. She felt exhausted and hollow. The operators congratulated her in quiet, professional ways. A nod. A handshake. A "nice work." She accepted them and moved on. Exhaustion stayed with her longer than when she was younger. She had earned this exhaustion.

She was preparing to go home for the first real sleep she had allowed herself in several days when her phone vibrated. It was her mother.

Callie answered immediately.

"Everything okay?"

"Yes," her mother said quickly. "The power flickered about ten minutes ago. Then it stayed on."

Callie leaned gently against the cold wall outside the control room.

"That's good, mom."

"The furnace kicked on, the house is starting to warm." her mother continued with an air of sadness. "The maple looks different in the light."

Callie closed her eyes.

"Different how?"

"Smaller, more sickly," her mother said.

She was wearing her feelings on her sleeve. Callie said nothing for a moment.

"Are you coming home tonight?" her mother asked.

"No," Callie said softly. "Not tonight."

After she hung up, she remained in the corridor longer than necessary. For the first time since the collapse, there were no breakers to close, no transformers to energize, no diesel trains to stabilize. Only space. And in that space, the weight was now settling. Rest was imperative.

Back in Harrisburg, Fred Samson, MidAtlantic's Chief Communications Officer returned with the draft language for an afternoon press conference. He had all the right words in the correct order. "Resilience, regional cooperation, unprecedented meteorological severity." He ended with the expected, "Infrastructure modernization initiatives already underway."

Langford scanned the talking points to ensure every sentence was accurate, and every sentence was complete.

Outside, the Susquehanna moved beneath its fractured surface. Ice shifts without sound until it doesn't. Another storm was building, and it wasn't weather related.

Callie stepped into her car and remembered she didn't filled out the night order book for her operators. She slipped quietly back into the control room to write the evening instructions. Her phone lit-up.

It was her mother again. She thought that was odd, they had just talked a few minutes earlier. After answering, Callie immediately sensed controlled panic in her voice.

"Callie… Your dad's on the ground."

The room instantly constricted.

"What do you mean on the ground?" She said quickly.

"We were outside," her mother said, breath uneven. "Clearing branches. He said he was fine, but he turned pale. Then he sat down and said his chest hurt. He wouldn't let me call at first. Then he just laid down right there and now he is struggling to breathe!"

Callie was already moving.

"Is he conscious?"

"Yes."

"Is he breathing normally?"

"I don't know what normal is anymore."

"Call 911. NOW. I'm leaving. Keep me posted."

She didn't remember grabbing her coat. She barely remembered telling her operators she was leaving. Sentinel Creek was seven hours from Millstone Junction. Seven hours of interstate. Seven hours of snowbanks and salt haze and exhausted plow trucks. Worse. Seven hours of guilt knowing she should have been there.

She called her mom several times, but the calls didn't go through. With every failed call her worry deepened. She stopped twice to get coffee. She was running on sheer exhaustion.

Finally, after four hours into the drive her phone lit up. It was her mom.

"Callie, the emergency room has been packed with people. We were here for over two hours when his chest pain worsened. They rushed him into the cath lab a few minutes ago."

"Mom, please let me know what is happening when you hear something. I am on my way."

What takes over when the stream of adrenaline depletes? Grit? Raw fortitude? She had been running on empty too long. The fear, the guilt, the thought of losing either of her parents became overwhelming.

She began to tear. The tears advanced to heaving sobs, before long she was struggling to see the road. She pulled over. She did not ever remember crying this hard.

"Callie, straighten up!" She screamed at the red-faced, swollen-eyed girl in the rear-view mirror. "Callie get a grip!"

The crying subsided to hiccupping sobs. She eased the car back onto the road. Her nose was running uncontrollably. She was shaking her head.

The phone lit up again.

"Mom?" She cried into the phone.

There was a pause.

"Callie? Are you okay? This is Dale."

She froze. She assumed it would be her mom. She took a gulp of air and tried to settle her spasmodic breathing.

"Dale, sorry, I thought you were my mom. They took my dad to the hospital with serious chest pains. I am trying to get to Springdale General Hospital now."

"Callie, I am so sorry." With surprise in his voice he continued, "You are back in your car again heading this way?"

She tried to hide her emotion.

"Yes. I need to be there."

"Have you gotten any sleep at all?"

She fought back another wave of tears.

"No. I am fine."

"You shouldn't be driving this alone."

She almost laughed.

"I've been doing everything alone."

Another silence.

"Callie, please be careful. Can I help in any way?"

"No, but thanks. Dale I have to go. I will talk to you later."

She could not stay on the phone with him. She could not handle any more.

The Springdale hospital emergency department had just shut down their diesel generator and transferred back to grid power. All the lights were on and the rooms were warming. When she walked into the waiting area, Dale was sitting next to her mother. He was holding her hand in his. Both immediately stood when they saw her. Her mother was surprisingly stoic.

"He's still in the cath lab," she said. "They think it was a heart attack. I haven't heard anything yet."

Callie nodded, but the nod carried no authority. The waiting room clock advanced in stubborn increments. Callie sat between Dale and her mother. After arriving at the emergency room, Dale determine who her mother was by family resemblance. He introduced himself, and comforted her. They made small talk until Callie arrived.

An almost frantic announcement was made over the hospital PA system laced with “code blue, code blue” causing her mother to tear up.

“I told him to leave it alone,” her mother said quietly. “The yard. The branches. But he said he wasn’t going to let the storm win.”

That sounded exactly like him. Callie squeezed her mother’s hands between her own frigid hands.

“I should have been here.”

“You were doing something important.”

“So was he,” Callie said.

The words came before she could stop them.

Her mother looked at her.

“I don’t know what I would do,” she whispered. “Forty-seven years.”

Callie felt something inside her give way. Not break. But give. She had spent the last three days preventing collapse. Preventing failure. Preventing loss of life in abstract numbers. But she had not been here when her father stepped into the cold to lift a branch heavier than he should have. She leaned forward and let the tears come quietly.

"I keep restoring power everywhere except the places that matter," she said.

Her mother squeezed her hand.

"It all matters," she replied. "That's the problem."

Dale offered quiet support. He knew not to interfere with the healing process. He knew just being there was making a difference.

30 minutes later, the cardiologist came and talked to them. He used phrases like "significant blockage" and "stent placed" and "damage but not catastrophic."

Her father would live. But he would never clear storm debris again without help. The margin had narrowed. Not eliminated. But narrowed.

When her dad emerged from the cath lab, he tried to make light of it.

"I told her it was indigestion from that questionable chili she made over the fireplace."

Callie smiled and took his hand.

"Dad, you don't get to fix this one yourself."

He smiled faintly.

"You always were kind of bossy."

Dale smiled broadly. For the first time in days, Callie laughed. And then cried again.

They kept Callie's dad in the hospital the next day and night. Callie stayed with her mom. She slept soundly for the first time in days. It was deep, dreamless sleep as her body strained for redemption in the warmth of her childhood bedroom.

When she awakened, she had missed several calls, including two from Dale. He didn't leave a message. She dialed him back over a cup of coffee. Seeing it was her, he answered on the first ring.

"Hey, Callie. How's your dad doing?"

"Good, Dale. What's happening?"

"First of all, I hope you got some rest. You needed it in the worst way."

"I did. No question about it."

He thought for a minute.

"The Setab lines are out for a while, but the recovery is going well. There has been an outpouring of help from all the independent system operators. The MidAtlantic system is slowly coming back together."

His voice took on an air of concern.

"Did you receive a call from a senate staffer asking questions about the storm and the blackout?"

"Dale, I am not even sure how long I have been asleep, but it appears I have missed several calls. I haven't listened to my messages yet."

"Callie can we have dinner again? There is a lot we must discuss."

She looked at her mom sitting quietly at the kitchen table.

"Of course. I would love that, but can I call you back in a bit?"

"No problem. Let me know."

They hung-up. Before she could say anything, her mom smiled broadly.

"Honey, for heaven's sake, go to dinner with that amazing man!"

Callie did a double take.

"How did…"

Her mother cut her off.

"I could hear him. More than this, I could see the look on your face, girl. You need to call that man back and go to dinner with him!"

Callie went over and hugged her mother affectionately.

"Thanks mom. I love you."

"Love you too, girl." She paused with a mischievous grin. "Am I going to get a grandbaby from this?"

Callie shook her head partially in embarrassment and partially disgust.

"Oh, mother, what am I going to do with you?"

Callie called Dale back and confirmed dinner that night at the diner in Millstone Junction.

That evening Dale picked Callie up at her folks' house. They were excited about seeing each other during a moment when drama wasn't high. Unfortunately, turned out it was. Dale had not burdened Callie with a new issue that had arisen just prior to her dad's heart attack.

After being seated at their table, Dale decided to forego small talk. He looked at Callie and gave her an odd smile.

"Callie, yesterday I got a call from a senate staff clerk. She was asking a lot of hard questions about MidAtlantic and the storm. She wants to do a deposition from you and I, and apparently several others. Did you hear anything about this?"

Callie was taken by surprise.

"No, I never heard from anyone, but the last three days have been a blur, and I do know that I missed a lot of calls."

Dale stared at her for a moment.

"I don't know if this is a witch hunt, or what. I have already decided that whatever I am asked, I will be completely honest with my answers."

"If they want to ask me questions, I will do the same."

They just stared at each other for a minute or so, the events leading up to the storm and the storm itself flooding both of their minds. Dale finally shook off the storm and reached across the small, two-top, diner table and took Callie's hand.

"I cannot tell you just how much I wish we lived closer to each other." His cheeks flushed slightly. "I think I…" He panicked and paused for just a moment. "I think I have grown extremely fond of you."

She sensed his panic and smiled a coy smile.

"I can honestly say that the feeling is mutual, Dale."

He smiled.

Amidst the din of dishes, utensils clattering, laughing, talking, phones, and bells permeating the diner that night, Callie and Dale had a quiet, intimate dinner. They didn't see or hear anything but each other.

Dale returned Callie to her folks house at about 9:00 pm, but they sat in the pickup and talked until almost midnight. He walked Callie to the door. Their kiss was passionate, repeating, and followed by a lengthy, emotional embrace. They both knew what was happening.

The next morning a senate staffer called Callie.

"Callie McGraw?"

"Speaking."

"Callie, my name is Julie Brady. I work from Bill Halcott's senate office. We would like to do an informal deposition concerning the recent failures on the power grid. Would this be possible?"

Callie thought for a moment.

"Why are you calling me?"

"We understand you are the power plant manager for the Sentinel Creek plant in the MidAtlantic system, and we have been told that you were a key planner in the black start arena. Is this not the case?"

"I was involved. I don't know that I was a key figure."

"Are you refusing the deposition?"

"Not at all. I just don't know how I could be of help."

"We would like to discern this for ourselves. When would be a good time to meet?"

"I am not at Sentinel Creek. My father had a serious medical issue and I am here in Millstone Junction for a few more days."

"Absolutely perfect!" She replied with enthusiasm. "I am in New Bedford. Can we meet in the conference room at the New Bedford Hilton anytime today or tomorrow?"

The New Bedford Hilton was only about 45 minutes from Callie's folk's house.

"That would be fine. Today would work best."

Later that afternoon, Callie sat calmly, confidently in the conference room. There were no cameras. There were three senate staffers including Julie. All of them were in their late twenties or early thirties. None looked hostile. That put Callie at ease.

They introduced themselves with careful politeness. Their laptops were open and their recorders and microphones were placed in the center of the table.

"This is informal," Julie said. "No oath. No transcript unless we proceed further."

Callie nodded.

"I don't need a transcript to tell the truth."

That earned the faintest glance between two of them. Julie folded her hands.

“Ms. McGraw, we’re trying to understand whether the grid failure was purely meteorological or whether operational decisions contributed.”

“It was meteorological,” Callie said evenly. “Ice accumulation exceeded design loading on multiple 230, 345, and 500 kV structures. Towers failed. When structures fail, lines go down.”

A staffer typed quickly, trying to keep up.

“And winterization?” he asked.

“Generation winterization is different from structural hardening,” Callie replied. “Our generating units performed. The transmission corridors failed first.”

“You attest that the generating units performed, but it has just come to light that one of the two nuclear plants operated by MidAtlantic was in danger of a meltdown. Is this true?”

Callie was caught off guard.

“Meltdown is a strong word. I don’t think the situation was that dire.”

"But you do agree that Torlon Hills nuclear had a nuclear emergency."

"Potentially, it could have been, but backup systems were in-place and functioned to prevent an actual emergency. The unit 2 reactor was in a safe shutdown state but still requires decay heat removal. This was never lost."

The senate staffers looked at each other with concern.

"Please correct our understanding, if necessary, but we were told that a major electrical transformer catastrophically failed and shut the plant down." She looked directly at Callie. "We were given pictures of the fire and aftermath. It certainly appeared to be an emergency to us."

"The transformer failure was unrelated to the decay heat removal situation."

"So you agree, there was a serious situation.?"

Callie winced. Now it appeared to be a witch hunt. She didn't want to be part of this.

“Julie, as far as I know the NRC has been notified and they will have an exhaustive investigation into the situation at Torlon Creek. I do not work there; I am not involved with the nuclear side of the company.”

Julie continued, undaunted.

“Callie, we were explicitly told that you were instrumental in the power restoration at Torlon Hills, yet you say you are not involved with the nuclear side of MidAtlantic Energy.”

Callie was growing concerned.

“I was directly involved with the restoration of station service electrical power at Torlon Hills. My job as a plant manager at Sentinel Creek involves the black start capabilities of the company. This was my role in this blackout. I was not at Torlon Hills during this incident.”

The staffers all took notes.

“Callie, let’s move back to the power grid. Were you aware of any hardening projects that were deferred?”

"I don't manage transmission capital," she said. "That would be Kendall Allen's department."

Julie tilted her head slightly, and glanced at the other two staffers.

"But as a plant manager, did you ever express concern about grid fragility?"

Callie considered that carefully.

"Every engineer expresses concern about fragility. That's our job."

"Specifically?"

"Specifically, I've always believed margins are not decorative."

Silence.

Julie leaned forward slightly.

"When you say margins are not decorative, what do you mean?"

"I mean redundancy is expensive," Callie said. "But physics is more expensive."

Another glance between staffers.

One of them shifted.

"Did corporate leadership ever pressure you to reduce maintenance scope or alter operational reserves?"

"No."

That answer came without hesitation.

Julie studied Callie's face.

"No?"

"No."

"You're certain?"

"I don't operate under pressure," Callie said calmly. "If someone asked me to do something unsafe, I would simply decline."

"And did anyone?"

"No."

That was true.

The staffers adjusted.

"Ms. McGraw," Julie said, softer now, "in your professional opinion, could this blackout have been prevented?"

Callie did not answer immediately.

She thought of her father on the frozen ground.

Of 500 kV towers folded in white fields of ice.

Of the Twin-Pac hunting frequency at fifty-eight hertz.

Of the diesel train – A at Torlon Hills flooded with glycol.

Of operators who had not slept.

"It could have been mitigated," she finally said. "Prevention implies certainty. This was a low-probability, high-impact event."

"Low probability," the younger staffer repeated.

"Yes."

"Were those risks documented?"

"I assume so. Good engineers try and document as much as possible."

"Were they acted upon?"

"That depends who you ask," she said.

That was the first answer that carried weight.

Julie caught it.

"What does that mean?"

"It means risk assessments exist in every system," Callie replied. "Whether they are funded is a different conversation."

Silence settled again. Julie closed her laptop halfway.

"One last question," she said. "If you were asked under oath whether capital allocation priorities influenced grid resilience, how would you answer?"

Callie met her eyes without blinking.

"I would answer the question exactly as written," she said. "No more. No less."

"And what would that answer be?"

Callie leaned back in the chair.

"Capital allocation and budgets *always* influences resilience."

The air in the room changed. Not dramatically, but perceptibly.

Julie closed the laptop completely this time.

"Thank you, Ms. McGraw."

"No cameras?" Callie asked.

"Not today."

Callie stood.

"For what it's worth," she added, "this wasn't a villain story. It was a margin story."

Julie's expression did not shift.

"That," she said quietly, "is exactly what we're trying to determine."

As Callie was walking into the parking lot of the hotel, Dale pulled in. She waited until he parked and met him halfway to the hotel entrance. They had a quick embrace.

"Everything good?" Dale asked quietly.

"Straight forward questions for me. I don't know what they will ask you. Dale, someone is feeding them. They claim to have pictures of the GSU fire and some of the damage at Torlon Hills. They seemed to have a lot of inside information."

Dale gave her a quick side-hug, and said, "I guess we'll see now."

They walked into the lobby together, but not side by side. The embrace faded into professional distance before the doors opened.

Julie Brady was already seated at the far end of the conference room.

"Mr. Morrison," she said, standing.

"Senate staff," Dale replied with a nod. "I was told this would be informal."

"It is," she said. "For now."

They began without preamble.

"Mr. Morrison, at any point during the weather event was Torlon Hills at risk of losing decay heat removal capability?"

Dale did not hesitate.

"Yes."

The word landed harder than Callie's had.

Julie looked up from her notes and over at the other staffers. The tone turned far more serious.

"Explain."

"We lost diesel back-up diesel Train - A. The Train - B was unstable for a period. Transmission corridors feeding station service were compromised. Had Train B failed before Franklin stabilized, we would have entered escalating emergency procedures."

"Were you comfortable with the redundancy available?"

"No."

Another pause.

"Was that redundancy historically sufficient?"

"Historically," Dale said carefully, "the transmission system was considered robust."

"Considered by whom?"

"By planning standards."

"By corporate leadership?"

"By engineering committees."

Julie leaned forward slightly.

"Were you ever directed to reduce hardening measures?"

"No."

"Were capital projects deferred?"

"Yes."

The room went still.

"By you?"

"No."

"By whom?"

Dale did not shift in his chair.

"Any transmission capital decisions are not within my authority."

"That wasn't the question."

Dale held her gaze.

"They were not within my authority."

The line was drawn.

Julie adjusted her pen.

“In your professional opinion, Mr. Morrison, did capital allocation priorities influence the severity of this blackout?”

Dale paused longer than Callie had.

He thought of Train A’s flooded bearings.

Of the Twin-Pac maintenance issues and operating on borrowed time.

Of watching the essential bus flicker.

Of hearing the word “code blue” in a hospital hallway hours later.

“Yes,” he said finally.

“In what way?”

Dale searched for the right words.

“The transmission system used to be one of the safety layers,” Dale replied. “During the storm it wasn’t. When one layer weakens, everything behind it carries more risk.”

Julie and the staffers continued taking extensive notes.

"Mr. Morrison, is it true that there was a catastrophic failure of a major transformer at Torlon Hills?"

"Yes."

"Can you tell me what caused this?"

"The Buchholz relay actuated when there was a pressure surge in the transformer, presumably from internal arcing that produced hydrogen and acetylene gasses. These gasses ignited. The cause of the arcing is unknown at this time."

"In your opinion, could the transformer failure have been prevented?"

Dale turned his head away for a moment and then looked directly at Julie.

"That question is incredibly simplistic. I will not be condescending, but this should be left to the experts."

The staffers all looked at each other.

"Mr. Morrison, we were provided documentation that clearly stated that transformer has had issues for at least three years, but maintenance was deferred. As the plant manager, can you tell me why maintenance was deferred?"

Dale cringed slightly.

"*Former* plant manager, Julie. And, yes, I can say that there was an extensive monitoring program in-place for that transformer, but the maintenance itself was deferred."

"Why?"

"Capital allocation."

"Why would you defer maintenance when you knew there was a potential for a catastrophic failure?"

"It was not my decision to defer maintenance. I already stated that transmission capital decisions were not within my authority."

The staffers all looked at each other again. One of them nodded his head to Julie.

"Mr. Morrison, I think this is all we require today. We appreciate you taking this time."

Callie and Dale left the hotel without speaking much. There was no triumph in either of them.

They spent the afternoon walking the city in cold sunlight, stopping for coffee, talking in fragments. Not about the Senate, or Kendall. They discussed smaller things like books, and old mistakes. What they had missed in earlier versions of themselves. In contrast to the drama of the storm, their souls were at peace.

Callie noticed she was no longer guarded around him. That surprised her. After her divorce, she had built her boundaries carefully. With Dale, they were thinning without effort.

He had blamed himself for Carla's distance for years. Quietly. Privately. He was beginning to see that some departures were not betrayals but misalignments. He marveled that on their best days he was not as comfortable with Carla as he was now with Callie.

By evening, neither of them wanted the day to end. They never uttered the word love. They didn't need to. The distance between Sentinel Creek and Silver Ridge remained unchanged. But it no longer felt abstract. It was a good day that day.

That next afternoon Dale received a call from Cal Johnson. It was brief.

“Dale, Cal Johnson.”

“Good afternoon, Cal.”

“I wanted to personally thank you for your leadership during the storm. Torlon Hills could have been far more complicated.”

“I appreciate that.”

A pause. Paper shuffling on the other end.

“With stability returning to the system, we’re transitioning facilities back to standard reporting structure. Effective immediately, you’ll return to Silver Ridge. Herman Distel will oversee Torlon until Marvin is able to resume as plant manager.”

Dale said nothing.

"We'll circulate the formal memo this afternoon," Cal continued. "This is simply a restoration of normal alignment."

Another pause.

"And Dale?"

"Yes."

"Your cooperation during this period has been noted."

The line clicked dead.

Dale called Callie immediately.

***

MidAtlantic Headquarters – Harrisburg

Over the next several weeks towers rose again across frozen fields. Crews arrived from neighboring systems. The grid slowly stitched itself back together. Many news outlets highlighted stories of the collaborative efforts from across the country. Dozens of human-interest stories emerged of human endurance, kindness and human resilience.

Stephen Langford spent an extraordinary amount of money in paid print and television advertising to convince the MidAtlantic service area customers how resilient, and responsive they were in the face of an "unprecedented weather event."

The crisis phase was over. The consequences phase was beginning.

At MidAtlantic headquarters in Harrisburg, the tone had shifted from operational to reputational. Stephen was working in his office when his admin assistant slipped into his office.

"There is a call on line – 2 from someone who says they are from the Office of the Senate Energy Committee. Would you like me to tell them you are not available?

Stephen thought about it for a moment. He knew these calls were in the pipeline. He pushed the button for line – 2.

"Stephen Lanford here."

"My name is Julie brady, I represent the office of the senate energy committee. We're compiling a preliminary briefing memo for members. We'd appreciate clarification regarding capital allocation decisions related to winterization and transmission hardening over the past five fiscal years."

Stephen did not react immediately.

"Clarification in what form?" he asked.

"Board-level summaries would suffice for now," Julie replied. "We're particularly interested in reclassification of resilience reserves and any associated risk assessments."

Reclassification. A careful word. He knew where this was going.

"Submit the request in writing," Stephen said evenly. "We'll respond appropriately."

"Of course," Julie replied. "We appreciate your cooperation."

The call lasted less than two minutes but it altered the temperature of the room.

Across the state line, in a tiny office of his comfortable, modest home, Harry Halvorsen did not make any calls. He did not send emails. He did not contact the press. He simply organized. Folders were opened. Digital copies were cross-referenced with archived board minutes. Executive incentive and bonus schedules were matched against capital deferrals. Risk assessments labeled "low probability" were highlighted, not for drama, but for context.

Harry was not angry. He was tired. Tired of systems that rewarded removal of margin. He closed one folder and opened another. There was no urgency in his movements. The storm had already completed the urgent part.

Harry had always been quiet, methodical, and focused. He worked extremely hard to get his Professional Engineer License. Being a P.E. opened countless doors for him. He had many job opportunities prior to choosing New England Power Cooperative.

Of all the careers he had options for, the cooperative suited him. They were not the highest salary. Not even close. But New England Power Cooperative was a non-profit and member owned utility. He knew he could make a difference there.

Harry was still arranging material at his desk when there was a knock at the door. It surprised him. He didn't get many visitors. He hesitantly opened the door and peered out.

It was Max Hillerbrand. They had worked together years earlier at New England Power Cooperative, back when systems were still maintained by people who expected to keep them for a long time. Max was almost 85 years old. Time had not been easy on him.

Harry attended the funeral for his wife, Bella, a month earlier. She had passed in the memory care unit of Sycamore Grove nursing facility. Her death certificate stated hypothermia as the cause of death. Most knew that Alzheimer disease was the greatest contributor.

"Max, how are you doing?"

Max gave a tired smile.

"Well enough to still be vertical. That's about the best I can offer."

"How did you get here?"

"My son, Ben, dropped me off. He will be back soon. He had a few errands to run."

Harry smiled, stepped aside, and let him in.

Max lowered himself slowly onto the couch.

"That storm really did a number on us," he said.

Harry nodded.

"It did a number on everyone."

Max looked around the room, then back at Harry.

"Way back when Buffton bought Northwind, I had a bad feeling. I never thought it would be this bad."

Harry nodded his head.

“It is difficult moving from a cooperative to an investor owned utility, that’s for certain.

Max’s eyes drifted toward the floor. His eyes watered.

“Harry, Bella’s gone.”

Harry stared at him.

“I know, Max. I was at the funeral.”

Max looked at Harry. He was confused. He then lowered his head.

“She was in the memory unit at Sycamore Grove.” Max swallowed. “They lost heat. Lost enough of it long enough. She didn’t make it.”

The words sat in the room.

Harry lowered himself slowly into the chair opposite him.

“I’m sorry, Max.”

Max nodded, but did not seem to hear him.

“She was going to die someday,” he said. “That’s not the part I can’t make peace with.”

Harry knew what he meant.

Max finally looked up.

"You always cared about the parts nobody else wanted to pay for. Margin. Reserve. All the things people called excess right up until they needed them."

Harry looked away.

"Max, it was out of my hands."

"Maybe," Max said. "But this still should not have happened."

They sat together after that with little more said. His son arrived a bit later to take him home.

Kendall Allen had not slept well in several days. He told himself it was the storm, the outages, the endless coordination calls. But the real reason sat deep in his mind. He kept replaying the scene where Stephen callously told him to ensure HR and the legal department were notified about Lewis Amboy's death. He couldn't shake it. He had considered this man his mentor.

Things worsened the day he read the deposition excerpts. He read them several times.

Dale Morrison: “Capital deferrals existed.”

Callie McGraw: “Capital allocation always influences resilience.”

Neither had accused him. That didn’t lessen the implications.

The lack of sleep was not playing well with Kendall. While normally upbeat, he was now moody. Withdrawn. Even angry.

He was in his office that morning working with Garrin Storz and the engineers to locate steel and components to continue the rebuild of the system when his phone rang.

“Mr. Allen, Stephen Langford would like to see you.”

He straightened his tie before standing. He had been in that office dozens of times for budget approvals, strategic reviews, and performance metrics.

He knocked once.

"Come in."

Stephen was not behind his desk. He stood near the window overlooking the river, hands folded behind his back.

"Kendall."

"Stephen."

There was no small talk. Stephen gestured toward a chair. Kendall sat, slowly, reluctantly.

"Have you read the preliminary summaries?"

"Yes."

"And?"

Kendall cleared his throat.

"They're oversimplifying a complex meteorological event."

Stephen nodded faintly.

"Yes. They definitely are."

For a moment there was a small light. Relief flickered in Kendall's chest. Stephen turned from the window.

"But they are not wrong about deferrals."

The relief evaporated.

"We reallocated within acceptable risk parameters, as you directed." Kendall said carefully. "Your modernization projects required capital discipline. Earnings targets were explicit."

"Explicit?" Stephen repeated calmly. "About dividends… Not about specific line items."

Kendall felt something ominous shift under his feet.

"It was understood," he said.

Stephen's gaze did not soften.

"Understood by whom, Kendall?"

Silence.

Kendall felt his own breathing. Stephen looked directly at him.

"You deferred Harbor substation hardening."

"Yes."

"You deferred secondary structural reinforcement on the eastern corridor."

"Yes."

"You signed those approvals, did you not?"

"Yes."

Each answer quieter than the last. Stephen walked back behind his desk and sat.

"Kendall, I hire intelligent, competent people to run their divisions."

Kendall nodded reflexively.

"I do not instruct engineers to compromise structural margin."

The words were sharp. They were precise. Kendall felt it like a knife. A numbness travelled through his face.

"We were protecting earnings stability," he said. "That was the priority, was it not?"

Stephen squinted slightly and studied him.

"My priority," he said evenly, "is dividend performance. That's what I am paid for."

A pause.

"Your priority was and is grid integrity."

There it was. No accusation. No anger. Just crystal clear separation.

Kendall felt the air thin.

"You're saying this is my responsibility."

"I'm saying," Stephen replied, "that you had authority over those decisions."

The room was shrinking. Kendall felt lightheaded.

"If I had told you to reduce structural resilience," Stephen continued quietly, "would you have done it?"

Kendall's mouth opened slightly, then closed. He knew the answer.

Stephen leaned back.

"I never asked you to reduce structural resilience."

That was the final moment, the moment Kendall now fully understood what was happening. While he had anticipated praise for efficiency, he had also interpreted silence as quiet approval. He had equated loyalty with alignment to purpose.

Stephen's voice softened almost imperceptibly.

"You realize the Senate Committee will ask who authorized the deferrals."

Kendall lowered his head and stared at the desk. His breathing was shallow.

"I did."

"Yes," Stephen said.

There was nothing else. There was no threat, no promise. Just inevitability.

Kendall left the office, slightly nauseous and in a fog. Life was surreal at this moment. He wanted to scream. He wanted to protest. Unfortunately, he now knew he was played by his own self-interests. This was not Stephen's fault. It was his. No one else was to blame. He didn't know what he would say to Stephanie. His kids. Anyone. He had never felt this alone, this isolated. Ever.

In the hallway, employees moved past him as they always had. Screens flickered with spreadsheets and databases. Phones rang. The system was stabilizing. His world was not. For the first time in his career, Kendall Allen understood the difference between meeting expectations and defending what mattered.

He had not been pushed. He had stepped forward. At this time, there would be no one else to absorb the impact. Stephen did not kill him. He had not been sacrificed. He had simply, willingly volunteered for execution.

That night he didn't sleep at all. He couldn't help but to think of his dad. An appliance repairman. A good appliance repairman. The man who occasionally fixed peoples' appliances for a loss, just to help them out. What would he think?

That next morning at breakfast, he sat and moved his food around the plate. He couldn't eat. Stephanie, his wife of 12 years, pulled a chair out, sat down, and staired directly at him for a few minutes.

"Kendall, what's going on?"

She turned stern.

"You've been saying it was the storm." She paused. "You haven't been eating. You haven't been sleeping. You've ignored the kids. This is not you, Kendall. What are you not telling me?" She stared at him, slowly shaking her head.

"Kendall, something must change. Something is not right. Talk to me please."

Kendall looked up. His voice was shaking. He was choking back tears.

"It was my fault, Steph. It was my fault."

"What was your fault?"

"Everything. The storm. The aftermath. I caused it."

She became alarmed. She had known Kendall 15 years and been his wife for twelve years. He was bold, almost arrogant. He was smart. He could be in the cage and stare down a hungry lion. This was not her husband.

"Kendall, weather happens. The weather was not your fault. What are you talking about?"

"Stephanie, I let my own ambitions destroy me and my career. I looked up to that man. I wanted to be that man. It now sickens me."

She instinctively knew he was talking about Stephen Langford.

"You still haven't told me why everything was your fault."

He angered slightly.

"I let him turn me into a product of his own miserable life. Without realizing it, I compromised everything I ever held dear. I thought I was a super-intelligent, highly effective manager." He shook his head angrily and raised his voice. "Steph, I was a dope. I was a pathetic, immature, arrogant puppet and it was no one's fault but my own."

“Kendall, I still don’t have a clue what you are saying. Make some sense of all this for me.”

“I remember as a kid in Sunday school.” He paused. “Pride cometh before a fall.” He kept shaking his head.

“Steph, I didn’t just fall, I lost everything.”

They stared at each other for another few minutes. She didn’t say a word.

“I have something I must do.” He finally said quietly as he got up from the table.

***

Part 16

Senate Hearings

****

The hearing room was cool and faintly drafty that morning. In the weeks after the storm, federal buildings had been restored. Critical infrastructure and visible districts were symbolic nodes. The Capitol complex hummed with quiet electricity while rural communities two hundred miles northeast still waited for permanent poles and wire.

Stephen Langford sat upright at the witness table, hands folded loosely, expression measured. To his left sat Calvin Johnson, Vice President of Nuclear, immaculate in a navy suit, composed and still. On his right sat Anthony Newson, Vice President of Fossil. The Vice President of Transmission and Distribution, Kendall Allen, was conspicuously absent.

Behind them were rows of staffers and cameras. At the far end of the table sat Harry Halvorsen. In front of him there was no stack of binders, nothing theatrical, just a thin leather folder. Several seats down sat Callie McGraw and Dale Morrison, quiet observers now. Teddy Warnick and Marvin Chandler were present as well, both outwardly composed.

The Committee Chair cleared his throat.

Harry Halvorsen was sworn in.

“Mr. Halvorsen, you served as Director of Systems Reliability and Grid Integration at MidAtlantic, correct?”

“Yes.”

“And you departed prior to the restructuring under Mr. Langford?”

“Immediately prior.”

“Why?”

Harry did not look at Stephen.

“Philosophical divergence.”

A faint ripple moved through the gallery.

“Explain.”

Harry folded his hands.

"The grid did not fail because of weather," he said calmly. "Weather was the catalyst. Not the cause."

Silence settled across the room.

"For the past decade, capital allocation shifted toward efficiency metrics. Structural redundancy, winterization margins, spare transformer inventories, and reserve assets were reclassified from resilience investments to underperforming capital."

He slid a single sheet forward.

"Each decision was legal. Each was defensible. Each improved quarterly financial reporting." He paused. "The system performed precisely as incentivized."

"Mr. Halvorsen, are you alleging misconduct?"

"No. I am alleging alignment."

"Alignment of what?"

"Incentives and outcomes."

He turned slightly.

"When resilience becomes optional, failure becomes predictable."

The Chair leaned forward.

"Margin?"

"Buffer," Harry said. "Space between operating condition and collapse. It is expensive. It does not show up as profit. It shows up as nothing happening."

He let that settle.

"Nothing happening is difficult to defend."

A few senators exchanged glances.

"Winterization budgets were trimmed. Quietly. Transformer spares were sold. Redundancy optimized." He closed the folder. "No one broke the law. No one intended harm."

He looked directly at the Committee.

"But intent is not the same as consequence."

Silence held.

"Mr. Halvorsen," the Chair said, "if no laws were broken, what are you suggesting we do?"

"Measure those things you value."

The room stilled.

"If resilience is not measured," he continued, "it will be optimized away."

No one interrupted him. No one needed to.

Harry was excused.

"The Committee calls Kendall Allen."

There was a subtle shift in the room. Staffers leaned forward. Cameras adjusted.

Kendall entered with Stephanie at his side. He looked thinner than he had only weeks earlier. Pale. Tired. He walked to the table without looking left or right.

He was sworn in.

"State your name for the record."

"Kendall Allen."

"You served as Vice President of Transmission and Distribution for MidAtlantic Energy?"

"Yes."

"You resigned approximately one month ago following the collapse of the grid?"

"Yes."

A pause.

“Mr. Allen, we’ve heard testimony regarding capital allocation, deferred hardening, and system vulnerability. We’d like to understand your role in those decisions.”

“I was responsible for transmission capital planning and execution.”

“Were projects deferred under your authority?”

“Yes.”

“Why?”

Kendall did not answer immediately.

“Because we could.”

A ripple moved through the room.

“We had models,” he said. “Load, weather probability, failure rates. Everything had a number attached to it. Risk was quantified. Prioritized. Scheduled.”

“And?”

“And we believed those numbers.”

“You’re suggesting the models were wrong?”

“No.”

He shook his head slightly.

"The models were accurate within the assumptions we fed them."

"And the assumptions?"

"They did not include what happens when multiple margins erode at the same time."

Silence.

"Were you aware of infrastructure that required reinforcement?"

"Yes."

"Did you defer any of those reinforcements?"

"Yes."

"Provide an example."

Kendall inhaled slowly.

"There is a transmission corridor northeast of Millstone Junction. 345 kV lattice suspension structures installed in the early 1970s." His voice lowered slightly. "I deferred it."

"Was that corridor considered high risk?"

"It was considered higher risk."

"By whom?"

"By me."

The room was still.

"Mr. Allen, are you aware that a fatality occurred on that line during the storm?"

"Yes."

"State the name."

"Lewis Amboy."

No one moved.

"Did your decision contribute to that failure?"

Kendall did not hesitate.

"Yes."

"Were you instructed to defer that project?"

"No."

"Were you pressured to do so?"

"No."

"Then why did you?"

"Because it fit the paradigm we were operating in."

"Explain that."

Kendall exhaled slowly.

"We measured financial efficiency," he said. "We rewarded it. We promoted it. We talked about discipline, optimization, return."

He paused.

"We did not measure margin the same way."

The Chair leaned back slightly.

"Where does responsibility lie, Mr. Allen?"

Kendall squeezed Stephanie's hand. He closed his eyes for a moment.

"With me."

The words did not sound like defense. Or confession.

Just quiet acceptance.

"Could this blackout have been prevented?"

"It could have been made far less severe."

"How?"

"By preserving margin."

"And why wasn't it?"

Kendall looked at the Chair.

"Because nothing happens when margin is preserved."

Silence filled the room.

"The chair recognizes a one-hour recess."

Callie and Dale moved into the large foyer outside of the auditorium. Harry Halvorsen pushed his way through the people to Dale. He carefully shook his hand.

"Dale, it's been a long time. How are you?"

Dale had not seen or talked to Harry for over three years. He only had met him on a couple of visits Harry made to Torlon Hills.

"Good, Harry. Powerful testimony in there."

"It needed to be said. There are some other things that should be said, but not here."

"I am sure you're right about that."

Harry locked eyes with Dale.

"You shouldn't have been moved out of Torlon Hills, Dale."

"What do you mean?"

"Being moved out of nuclear to Silver Ridge."

Dale wasn't sure what to say. He smiled weakly.

"I guess it could have been worse."

"You don't know what I am talking about, do you?"

Dale shook his head.

"I guess not."

"Dale, the fire at Torlon Hills during your infamous and partially televised tour wasn't a warehouseman's failure. It appears it was a systemic failure of the ADM software package."

"What are you talking about?" Dale had heard innuendo and hearsay, but nothing more than ungrounded speculation.

"Aegis Data Management systems software is seriously flawed. The NRC has several investigations underway at three other nuclear plants besides Torlon Hills.

Your warehousemen were not at fault. The peer review system didn't fail. They weren't lying during the investigation."

Dale thought for a moment before replying.

"I knew that the ADM software had issues, but the warehousemen should have caught the material issue on the o-rings. It is common knowledge that rubber o-rings quickly deteriorate when in contact with Fyrquel fire-retardant hydraulic fluid."

Harry shook his head slowly.

"Dale, you don't understand the level of issues with the ADM software. It appears to be designed to favor certain suppliers."

He paused.

"Suppliers that have financial stakes in the ADM platform. It is a potential house of cards that could be about to tumble and I think the fallout will hit several companies including MidAtlantic Energy."

Callie looked at Harry.

"Why does this affect Dale?"

"Dale's known competence may have been perceived as a threat to certain individuals in MidAtlantic. I speculate that he was conveniently moved out of Torlon Hills as part of a systemic damage control campaign."

Callie thought back to the system wide adoption of the ADM software. It was immediately after Stephen Langford appointed Cal Johnson as the VP of nuclear.

They continued to discuss ADM. Harry declined to name names. He just repeated that the issues went to the highest level of management in MidAtlantic Energy.

The recess ended and everyone returned to the auditorium for resumption of the hearings.

Immediately after the recess Teddy Warnick was called for testimony.

"Please state your name and your position within MidAtlantic Electric."

"Teddy Warnick. I am the plant manager of the Franklin Energy Center."

“Mr. Warnick, Franklin Energy Center is designated as one of two black start plants for the MidAtlantic Energy system. Is this correct?”

“Yes, that’s correct.”

“Mr. Warnick were there issues with the black start system at Franklin Energy Center during the recent storm?”

“Mr. Chairman, the storm was the issue. It was unprecedented. Concerning the black start system at Franklin, as far as I am concerned, it worked flawlessly.”

Callie looked at Dale with unbelief in her eyes. Dale shook his head and squeezed her hand under the table. Nothing more needed said.

Callie and Dale were eventually called for a repeat of the questions asked during the informal data gathering that took place much earlier at the New Bedford Hilton. There were no surprises.

Additional testimony followed over the course of the afternoon.

Some of it focused on procurement systems, material tracking, and software platforms used across multiple stations. Investigators described irregularities, substitutions that should not have been approved, records altered or misclassified, approval pathways adjusted in ways that were difficult to detect in isolation.

Those issues did not initiate the collapse. They had just narrowed margins further.

In several cases, it appeared individuals benefited from those decisions. Harry was right. The actions of several were under review. No single failure explained what had happened. That, more than anything, unsettled the room.

In the coming months, Stephen Langford was quietly removed as the CEO of MidAtlantic Energy.

Reconstruction continued. Reports were written. Charts were presented. The language was careful. The most common phrase remained "unprecedented meteorological severity."

Transmission corridors were rebuilt with heavier steel in certain stretches. Not everywhere. Everywhere was too expensive. But where towers had failed most visibly, replacements stood thicker against the horizon.

Some corridors were hardened. Some were not. Not every lesson held.

Months later, at Franklin Generating Station, the newly appointed plant manager, Callie McGraw, stood in her control room and watched a new operator struggle through a cold start.

She did not take the controls from him. He needed to feel it. The delay in pressure rise. The lag in valve response. The way systems resisted when margins narrowed.

Outside, the plant grounds were green. Equipment was repaired. Some of it improved. The aging Twin-Pac was in the process of receiving a controls upgrade.

Not everything was fixed. Everything never is.

Her father no longer lifted storm debris alone. He sat on the porch more often now, offering instructions no one requested. Her mother still complained about the maple. Callie visited often. She lived only an hour away now. She was much closer to Dale and the people who mattered.

Callie and Dale did not rush anything. They understood that forcing sequence can destabilize more than it repairs. Their bond continued to grow.

The next winter, capital requests included additional structural hardening along key 500 kV corridors. Not all were approved. Many were.

Margins widened in small, deliberate increments. Not enough to eliminate risk, but enough to delay it. No one declared victory. The grid continued as it always does.

Most people forgot the blackout within a year. The discomfort faded faster than the memory. But a few remembered the narrowing. The sound of steel under ice.

That improbable does not mean impossible.

They were not loud. They did not control capital. They did not write policy.

But they watched the margins.

Carefully.

They were the last people who still knew.

***

About the Author

Mark A. Gregg is the is the founder of SimGenics, LLC and Books Sphere, LLC. With more than four decades of experience in the electric power industry, he has commissioned seven large generating stations. Within SimGenics he has focused on the design, development, and deployment of high-fidelity simulator systems used to train operators at fossil, nuclear, and combined-cycle generating stations on every continent.

Over the course of his career, he has trained thousands of operators and engineers across major utilities throughout the world. He has worked extensively inside control rooms, dispatching centers, and generating stations during both normal operation and system disturbances.

The Last People Who Knew reflects observations drawn from a career spent working with complex systems, where performance depends as much on experience as it does on design.

www.ingramcontent.com/pod-product-compliance
Lightning Source LLC
LaVergne TN
LVHW100503110826
845146LV00002B/497

* 9 7 9 8 9 9 5 6 1 3 0 0 8 *